CLUB MAFIA – THE ANGEL
A DARK MAFIA ROMANCE

STELLA ANDREWS

COPYRIGHTED MATERIAL
COPYRIGHT © STELLA ANDREWS 2022
STELLA ANDREWS HAS ASSERTED HER RIGHTS UNDER THE COPYRIGHT, DESIGNS
AND PATENTS ACT 1988 TO BE IDENTIFIED AS THE AUTHOR OF THIS WORK.
THIS BOOK IS A WORK OF FICTION AND EXCEPT IN THE CASE OF HISTORICAL FACT,
ANY RESEMBLANCE TO ACTUAL PERSONS, LIVING OR DEAD, IS PURELY COINCIDENTAL.
ALL RIGHTS RESERVED. NO PART OF THIS BOOK MAY BE REPRODUCED OR
TRANSMITTED IN ANY FORM WITHOUT WRITTEN PERMISSION OF THE AUTHOR,
EXCEPT BY A REVIEWER WHO MAY QUOTE BRIEF PASSAGES FOR REVIEW PURPOSES
ONLY.

18+ THIS BOOK IS FOR ADULTS ONLY. IF YOU ARE EASILY SHOCKED AND NOT A FAN
OF SEXUAL CONTENT THEN MOVE AWAY NOW.

18+

NEWSLETTER

Sign up to my newsletter and download a free book

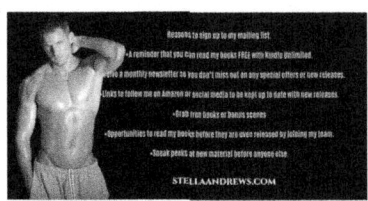

stellaandrews.com

CLUB MAFIA

THE ANGEL

The Angel

A dying man gave me the gift of life.
Two names.
One of them belongs to the mother I never knew I had.

When I found her, I wanted answers and something more.

Her stepdaughter.

Louisa Sullivan

The daughter of a billionaire, but it's not the money that interests me.
Finding my mother was only part of my plan.
I need Louisa for my own reasons and she is perfect.
Marry her and merge our families to bring her uncle down and set my friend free.

It turns out the other name holds the secret that will topple an empire, and I'm the man to release the wrecking ball.

Louisa

There's a stranger in our house.
As soon as I enter the room, I know who he is.

Two dark eyes watch me approach, and it's as if he is reading my soul.

He is the most handsome man I have ever met and yet there's an edge of danger to him that makes my skin prickle with energy and causes a shiver to fizz my blood with the promise that things will never be the same again.

I was right.
He brought with him chaos, destruction and power and what he wants most is—me.

Phenomenally dark, twisted, hot and delicious!
Scenes may upset some readers, you have been warned.
Bleeding romance and suspense, this book ticks all the boxes.

If you love a dark mafia romance, this series will have you begging for more.

PROLOGUE

FLYNN

It's the silence that sickens me. Enfolding me, choking me, threatening to end my life and free me from this madness. I can almost count every beat of my heart as I wait for it. The sense of a storm building that many will not survive. It's always there, a twisted promise of damnation because of him.

The scream shatters the silence as it always does. Piercing, terror filled and tortured.

Logan raises his eyes to the heavens as if there is any help there.

There is no one to help the poor unfortunate woman who has captured Wesley's attention tonight.

My nails pierce the skin on the palm of my hand as I try desperately to focus my mind on anything other than the horror unfolding behind the closed door.

I wish I could help her. I want to set her free, but that is out of my control for now.

A gunshot carries through the stone walls and Logan looks to the floor. My own eyes raise to the heavens in a silent prayer for her soul. She's at peace now. I must be grateful for that, at least.

Before I can catch my breath, a slight movement in the corridor catches me off-guard and on autopilot I draw my weapon.

Logan is still looking at the floor and doesn't react quickly enough, and as the shot rings out, I dive for cover as it hits the stone beside my head.

More gunshots follow as I roll to the side and take aim.

I can't be certain how many gunmen there are and fire at will, covering Logan, who is flat on the floor. Has he been hit? Is he dead? I almost pray for that myself, but the will to survive kicks in and my bullets find their mark.

As the gun smokes in my steely grasp, I pause and wait for more to follow. Nothing. Endless silence where death enters the room and admires a good day's work.

I crawl across to Logan and spin him on his back. The gaping wound in his chest tells me he doesn't have long.

The door remains closed as usual and as he gasps for air, I put pressure on the wound and whisper, "I've got you, Logan. Stay with me."

His hand reaches out and grasps my jacket in a surprisingly strong move and he pulls me down to his rasping lips.

"Promise me you will find Vivian Clark and Iris Young."

"What are you talking about?" I whisper my confusion and his eyes are wide and frantic as he gasps, "They will set you free."

"I'm sorry man, who are they?"

I'm confused and wonder if he's delirious and as he drags his final breath he whispers, "Your mother."

As his vacant eyes stare at me no more and he faces his sins, I am left with more questions than answers.

My mother, he said.

I never knew I had one.

For a moment I stare at my uncle's consigliere as if I'm dreaming. Then I glance past him and see the gunman on the floor, who appears to be fresh out of high school. Carefully, I lower Logan to the ground and close his eyes, whispering a prayer for God to have mercy on his soul. Despite everything, he was a good man and one of the few I admired. Then my attention reverts to the gunman and as I peer closer, my heart twists when I see the youthful face of a kid who was sent to do a man's work.

The door opens behind me and my uncle shouts, "What the fuck is going on? Is that Logan?" He sounds more angry than grieving and I snap, "The kid shot him."

Wesley heads across and kicks the corpse of the young man so it rolls on its back and spits in his face, saying cruelly, "Fucking amateur."

"I don't think Logan would agree with that."

I glare at my uncle, who doesn't even have the decency to pay his respects to his loyal consigliere, and he snaps, "Looks to be the girl's boyfriend. I was warned she had one."

I stare at the dead body and my heart breaks for him. He tried to save her, not knowing it was a fool's errand.

"How do you know?" I'm curious about that and Wesley shrugs, "She told me he would come for me, right before I fucked her to death."

It would be so easy right now. I am almost tempted to finish the job and place a well-deserved bullet right between his eyes, but I'm aware it would only gain me a moment's satisfaction before my own life was ended in a far more brutal way.

Wesley Vasquez has the best protection there is courtesy of Massimo De Lauren. His best friend, brother from another mother, and his closest ally in the world. If I dispose of one, I will face the other and even though it's certain that time will come, it's not now.

Wesley takes his own gun and delivers a parting shot

through the kid's skull and laughs as his brains redecorate the stone walls around us.

Then he looks around and sighs. "Fucking Logan. He should have seen that coming. You sleep, you die."

Then he says almost as an aside. "He should have been better than that."

I cast my eyes on the most loyal servant my uncle ever had and feel betrayed on his behalf. He doesn't deserve to be dismissed as somehow at fault for this, and I say evenly. "Shall I call the clean-up crew?"

"No need."

Wesley almost looks irritated as he growls, "We'll torch the place. Explain it as a freak accident. Nobody will ever discover we were here, anyway, and if they did…" He laughs wickedly, "They won't live to ask their dumb questions."

As Wesley heads back down the hall to the boiler room, I am almost tempted to send him to hell in his own inferno, but Logan has rattled me. Two names. Why two and who are they?

There's something in the back of my mind that tells me I need Wesley alive until the mystery is solved and so I hold those names in my memory like the most precious cargo because one of them belongs to my mother and it's a meeting that's been a long time coming.

LATER THAT NIGHT when the house sleeps, I pull out my cell and text the man I trust with the two names that are burning a hole in my sanity. If there is anything I need to know about them, I trust Baron to deliver the information to my eyes only. He is one of five men I trust with my life and the only ones who are in this madness with me. We are five brothers by choice and one by earning our respect. Baron always sat on the edge of our group in college and yet when it counted, pledged his loyalty to Club Mafia. For some reason, Baron knows shit and is the perfect man to trust with my newfound knowledge.

I could go to Malik as we always do, but for some reason Baron's was the first name to come to mind. There is something deliciously sinister about our tight-lipped friend and just for now, I want to keep this news from the others.

As I wait, I wrap the shadows around me of the early hours and feed off them. This is the time I love the most. Alone and free, at least until the dawn breaks and hell wakes up for another hit on my soul. I've always loved solitude. It's where I am most at peace and as I wash the grit of the day from my memory, only one word lingers like the purest sensation on my tongue. I have a mother. But which one is she?

It could be an hour or even three, but the text returns quicker than expected. Does that man never sleep?

A wry smile twists my lips as I sense an affinity with our secretive friend. Always there, watching from the shadows and offering words of advice when needed.

However, only two words are contained in this text, and they create more questions than answers.

Dimitri Sullivan

I sigh and silently curse my enigmatic friend. Fuck Baron. Why can't he speak in sentences like any normal person?

Now I have three names and I'm none the wiser, so with a frustrated sigh, I turn to my preferred search engine to help me.

As I read the information from the mighty web, I sense an excitement stirring deep in my core. It turns out that was the only name I needed, and my mission is set. First stop Club Mafia to check in with my brothers and then a plane bound for Seattle and a very interesting conversation at the home of Dimitri Sullivan.

CHAPTER 1

FLYNN

THREE WEEKS LATER

*A*s the plane touches down at Seattle airport, the smile on my lips was put there by the thought of Wesley wondering where the fuck I've gone.

It's not unusual for me to take off. He knows me by now, but I have been gone for one week already and my phone is lit with abusive texts and threats from the bastard himself.

As the commercial jet taxis to the stand, I dash out a reply and hit send with a soft laugh.

I'm on vacation, uncle.
I'll text you when I'm home.

The fact it's not unusual buys me more time and I'm guessing he's given up trying to understand me by now. I know I frustrate him, and the bastard is deluded if he thinks I can't look after myself and is probably thinking I've hooked up with a chick in Bora Bora or something.

I probably only have one more week at the most before his patience runs out and so I need to act fast.

If I'm nervous at all, it doesn't show and as I grab a cab and rattle off the address, only his raised eyebrows tell me he's impressed.

I'm guessing he doesn't get many customers heading to Denny-Blaine, and certainly not one looking like me.

I can't help the threatening aura I dress in every morning. I shrug it on when I reach for my gun. I get that I intimidate people, hell I make a career of it, and I hide behind the mask of 'don't fuck with me' because I prefer it this way. Now I'm wondering if I should tone it down a little. The woman I have come to see may not appreciate the fuck off attitude and dark smoldering eyes. I'm guessing she's used to a different kind of visitor, and yet how can I pretend to be something I'm not? This is who I am, not who I want to be, and I need her help to see if there is anything worth salvaging in this sorry carcass that was inflicted on the world courtesy of her womb.

We reach the outskirts of the neighborhood they live, and it's as if the air is fresher here, with more oxygen, pure even. As the houses grow in size and are surrounded by parkland, I can tell my mother has fallen on her feet at least. I should be resentful of that, but until I've heard her story, I'm happy for her. I'm hoping she has a good explanation for what happened to me and I'm not sure I can deal with hearing she gave me up willingly.

All my life I've lived with rejection, pain, and loneliness. Me against the world until I met my brothers at college and finally found a place I belonged. Do I belong here with her? I'm pretty nervous about that and as the car rolls into the driveway and stops short of huge wooden gates, I experience a moment's doubt that I did the right thing in showing up here at all.

The driver lowers his window and presses the intercom and

my mouth dries as he looks over his shoulder and barks, "Your name?"

I'm not a man who is prone to panic attacks, but now seems a good place to start and my voice doesn't even sound like mine as I whisper, "Flynn Vasquez."

Now I feel like a fool because why the fuck would they let me in and as he speaks the words, I curse my own stupidity.

I hear the voice on the intercom say sharply, "Wait there. Someone will be out to speak with you."

And my heart sinks. This may prove more difficult than I thought.

I watch as a side gate opens, and the security guard appears, staring with suspicion in my direction.

Trying hard to appear normal, I smile and step out of the cab.

"Hi, um, they aren't expecting me, but I'm here to see Vivian Clark."

"You're not on the list."

He looks bored, unconcerned even, and I nod. "I know. It's just, well, it's very important that I see her. If you could maybe just pass a message on, I would be grateful."

"What message?"

The guy looks bored already and I say quickly, "Could you tell her that I was sent by Iris Young?"

He nods and heads back the way he came and I'm hoping like hell this gamble will pay off.

The cab driver throws me a pitying look which doesn't make me feel any better about things and it seems like an eternity before the guy heads back and regards me with a different expression from the one before.

"Follow me."

The cab driver whistles, and I am so astonished, I grasp a bunch of dollar bills and hand them to him, muttering my thanks.

As I head through the gate, my heart thumps because now I'm here, I'm not even sure what I'm going to say.

We walk up a path flanked by flowering shrubs and home to ornamental lighting that must be amazing at night. In fact, this place gets more impressive by the second as a billionaire's world opens up before my eyes.

I'm used to fancy living. My uncle demands it, but this is something else. This wasn't paid for by broken bones and blasted brains. This wasn't the product of another person's misery or a drugs deal. This is what hard work, and a lot of luck gets you and even the air tastes clean without the ghosts of the damned circling as you live in the shadow of their misery.

I take a huge draft of fresh, honest air and wonder if it's something I might experience in my future. Probably not, but I can dream at least and as I follow the security guard through a door in the side of an outbuilding, I wonder what the next hour will bring.

First, I am made to surrender any weapons and I almost laugh as I lay the gun on the table, followed by my hunting knife.

He looks surprised, and I grin ruefully.

"Sorry. I take my right to bear arms seriously; you need to where I come from."

He looks a little worried, and for some reason I want to reassure him.

"Listen, I'm here for information and mean nobody any harm. It's a little delicate, but I promise I won't cause a scene."

Maybe he believes me when his expression softens a little as I try to dilute the menacing edge I wear so well and appear like any normal person for once.

He asks me to fill in a form with my contact details and it's as if I'm applying for a job and in a sick way, I suppose I am. The job of Vivian Clark's son. I wonder if she has a vacancy.

It takes thirty minutes to bypass security, and the guard escorts me to a room on the other side of the courtyard.

It remains separate from the house and looks to be an office of sorts and he points to a seat set around a low-slung table.

"Mrs. Sullivan will meet you here. You have five minutes."

I watch as he retreats to a seat set against the wall and I sigh inside. Part of me is happy she has security and part of me resents it. I mean her no harm. Even if I don't like what I hear, I will be richer for it.

The clock ticks down to the most important meeting of my life and, as I wait, I set my mind accordingly. Despite my personal reason for coming here, I still have a job to do and marriage into this family will assure us of the strongest allies.

Despite everything, I can't fail my brothers and so if things don't go according to our strategy, I will just have to suck it up and revert to Plan B.

CHAPTER 2

FLYNN

The door opens and I hold my breath. This is it. I can't quite believe that I'm here at all and yet as the woman steps inside, I take a moment to catch my breath.

I stand as if in a trance because it's undeniable. The resemblance is too striking because for the first time in my life, I am looking at an older, female version of myself.

She steps back as if I physically assaulted her and her hand flies to her mouth as she struggles to understand what's happening.

I have no words and for the first time in my life, an overwhelming surge of emotion renders my usually cool façade broken at my feet. Tears glisten in my eyes as I stare at the woman who gave me life, and I am in no doubt about that. Vivian Clark is my mother and I already know that before any DNA test is demanded.

For the longest moment, we stand staring at one another as if we're in a different time zone. The security guard fades into my subconscious as I stare at a woman I never believed existed.

She appears to shake herself before stepping forward and

gazes at me as if I'm a hallucination and as the guard shifts nervously, she whispers, "Leave us."

"Ma'am, I must insist…"

"Leave us—now!"

Her command is final, and he nods, looking unhappy, but does as she asks and as the door closes softly behind him, she approaches me with tears in her eyes.

"What is your name?"

A simple question that seems odd on this occasion and I whisper, "Flynn."

"They told me you died at birth."

The shock of that hits me like a gut punch and the anger builds as I sense my life is built on a lie.

"They were wrong."

I blink because I never considered for one moment she would accept me as her son without question. I accepted she would be suspicious and deny everything, but it's as if somehow, she knew me on sight. That means more to me than anything, and I choke back emotion as I stare into a pair of identical eyes to mine.

"How did you find me?"

Her words are measured, but her breathing is erratic, and I say slowly, "Your name fell from the lips of a dying man. Logan, my uncle's consigliere."

She takes a step backward. "Mafia."

She exhales sharply and I sense her retreating away from me and I say desperately, "I'm afraid so."

Her eyes fill with tears, and she whispers, "I wish I had known you, Flynn. I wish I had the chance to love you."

I watch with morbid fascination as the tears run from her eyes while she stares at me as if she's been starved of sight her whole life. It is overwhelming and I feel strangely exposed witnessing such pure emotion. In fact, I've never seen anything like it and it's a lot to absorb.

She appears to shake herself and says with a stutter, "We need to work this out. Where we go from here. The future."

Her acceptance of the situation unravels me and I'm struggling knowing what to do and then something happens that breaks me apart and I'll never be the same again.

She shifts closer and takes my hands and whispers, "Do you believe in miracles, Flynn?"

"No." I sound bitter, defeated even, and I hate hearing it in my jaded voice.

"Then I believe enough for both of us. Thank you for finding me and if you agree, please stay for a while. I need to know everything about you and where you've been for your whole life."

I never expected this and for a moment I can't voice the words that are quivering in response to something I never expected to hear. Then she steps forward and pulls me close and as my mother's arms close around me, I can't stop the emotion from grabbing my heart and holding it hostage.

For so many years, a lifetime even I have dreamed what this would be like. A deep yearning in the soul of a lost boy who never experienced what it would be like to have his own mother hold him in her arms. A child who was starved of love and affection and cruelly abused every single fucking day of his life and just experiencing the unconditional love of a mother's arms, is a powerful thing to witness. She owns me already. Just that one simple act of love is enough to make me die a happy man because, for the first time in my life, it's as if I have a beginning and now possibly a better ending than I ever expected.

We stand in an embrace that is anything but awkward and as she pulls back, she smiles into my eyes and drags her finger down my face. "You are so handsome, Flynn. So perfect."

"I am far from perfect..."

I falter because I'm not sure what I should call her and she smiles and says in a gentle voice, "It's Vivian. Let's take this one step at a time; we have a lot of ground to make up."

She appears to regroup and says brightly, "We have a lot to discuss. My husband will be curious, and we should start with him."

"Will he mind?" I'm anxious about that, and she shrugs. "He will be suspicious, but as he knows my history, I doubt he will be surprised. He's a fine man, the best actually, and you have nothing to fear from him."

I'm a little surprised at that because, knowing his brother and the madness inside his head, I can't believe he could be so different and yet I keep my thoughts to myself and smile tentatively. "I would like to meet him. He sounds, a good man."

She takes my hand and smiles.

"Please excuse this formal meeting room. We should head into the house; you must be hungry."

I smile but am so blown away by her reaction to me, I follow her in a daze. It strikes me that this feels almost normal, as if I have always lived a regular life with a loving family. Is this what it's like? It's better than any high from any drug and I could become addicted. In fact, I already am.

CHAPTER 3

LOUISA

Sienna is seriously grating on my nerves, and I want her to leave, but if I make a scene, she will use it against me.

"Honestly, Louisa, you should loosen up a little. I mean, for God's sake, Ashton Michaels is the best you can expect, and I would have marched him up the altar before he could change his mind."

"Then it's a good job you're not me because I have expectations."

She laughs out loud. "You and your expectations. Word of advice, sis, you need to lower your standards. You're hardly the belle of the ball and the pickings are getting slimmer the older you get. In fact, you're known as being difficult and once a girl gets a reputation, it's all downhill from there."

"Are you here just to throw insults, or is there a reason for your visit?"

I lower my pen and sigh. As always, Sienna is bored and thinks baiting me is the best cure for that and she shrugs, sucking the lollipop in her ruby red lips noisily.

"I'm just saying you should snap up, Ashton. His father is

the head of a bank, for Christ's sake. You wouldn't have to…" She waves her arm at my books. "Work for a living. I mean, what's that all about, anyway? You're an heiress, not a pauper. You don't actually have to earn your own money, so grab a personal shopper and do what's expected of you. The future is bright, so open the drapes and let the sunlight in."

"Fuck off, Sienna, and go and work on your tan. You know absolutely nothing about me and don't pretend you care."

"You're a little touchy, aren't you? I was only trying to help."

She huffs and chucks the lollipop into the trash can and storms out, slamming the door behind her and leaving me in blissful solitude.

Focusing my attention back on the contract I'm reading, I try to empty my mind of useless frivolity. It's true I don't need to work, but I want to. Being a trophy wife is not a future I want for myself and I'm mindful that if I want to take over my father's business one day, I will need to be better than everyone else.

The door opens again, and I huff with exasperation. "I told you…"

"Louisa."

I straighten up as the abrupt tones of my father command my attention and he breezes inside and says casually, "I have a meeting tomorrow in town I want you to sit in on."

"Of course." I sit up and take notice because this is new. I may work for my father in a very junior capacity, but he's never involved me in a meeting before. The most I get to do is read through contracts and do the filing, so I wonder what's changed.

He wanders over to the window and, for some reason, looks a little disturbed.

"Is everything ok?"

"I'm not sure." He huffs and appears to focus on something outside.

Wandering across to the window, I stand beside him and see Emilio, his security guard, heading back to the gatehouse.

"What's the problem? Perhaps I can help."

"Doubtful, but the gesture is appreciated."

"Is it the business?"

I hold my breath because if the business is in trouble, that's big news and he laughs softly. "No, the business is strong. It's well, family matters."

I'm a little anxious because I'm family and Sienna's words are haunting me right now. I'm lucky that my father is supportive of my choices but the fact I've turned down every suitor has not gone unnoticed, but I never really thought it mattered. Now I'm not so sure.

"Is it me?" I sound anxious and he turns, his kind smile lighting up his face, putting my mind at rest in an instant.

"Of course not. You're possibly the only one I can count on around here."

"Sienna?"

He sighs and rakes his fingers through his hair in a gesture that scares me more than anything because my father doesn't do uncertainty, worry or anything that makes him out to be any less in control of all our lives.

"It's Vivian."

My heart lurches because I hope to God there isn't any trouble between them. Ever since Vivian came into my father's life, the world has been a much brighter place.

Sienna's mother was a bitch and used my father like an ATM. He was besotted by her and indulged her with everything she wanted, even turning a blind eye to her many affairs, just desperate to have her in his life. She was the proverbial gold digger, and their daughter is shaping up to be much the same. When she ran off with a movie producer who could offer her the Hollywood lifestyle she craved, I remember breathing a big sigh of relief and for a period I stepped into her shoes as the hostess and lady of the house. Then he met Vivian, and I was happy to step aside. Unlike his previous wife, she isn't interested in fame, money and being seen in the right places. All that matters to her is family life and making it amazing for us all, and if she has done something to burst the bubble, I am more fearful of that than anything.

"What's the problem with Vivian?"

He looks so troubled I wonder if she's ill. That can only explain the despairing glint in his eyes.

He shakes his head. "She has a visitor, and it may alter things around here."

"A visitor?"

"Yes, a man showed up at the gatehouse and asked to see her."

He exhales slowly. "Emilio ran a check on the guy, and it appears he's got connections I'm not happy about."

"Is Vivian in trouble? Danger even?"

I hold my breath and he merely shrugs, which is not the answer I was looking for.

"I'm not sure."

Now I'm really nervous and he turns and smiles and if he thinks that will reassure me, he's wrong.

"Maybe I should go and see for myself. I just wanted to tell you about the meeting and warn you that things may be a little different around here for a while."

"OK."

I watch him leave with the sense of a storm approaching. My father looked weary, as if he was resigned to something that he could do nothing about. As I glance out of the window, I wonder about the current visitor. Who is he and why is something telling me everything is about to change?

CHAPTER 4

FLYNN

This is the most surreal experience of my life. Vivian has welcomed me in, a stranger off the street, and claimed me as her son with no hesitation, which makes me wonder if she is telling me the truth. Did she really think I'd died, or did she know all along I was living with the monster under my bed?

Nothing is adding up, which raises my guard. I want to believe this is the stuff dreams are made of, but I've led a bitter life of disappointment and good things don't happen to me. Not ever, so I will proceed with caution and test the water before I dive in.

We head to a huge kitchen where a woman is working away, and she looks up with curiosity as we walk into the room. She stares at me in astonishment and her hand flies to her mouth as she whispers, "Well, I'll be…"

Vivian smiles and says with a slight tremble to her voice, "I have an, um, visitor. Mrs. Hedges, would it be possible to rustle up some lunch? He must be hungry."

"Of course, ma'am."

"Thanks, we'll be in the blue room. Make enough for three. Mr. Sullivan will be joining us."

"Consider it done."

Mrs. Hedges can't stop staring at me and Vivian whispers, "Even she can see the resemblance; it's uncanny."

"It is." I can't stop gazing at my mother and she is the same and then she surprises me by smiling gently and whispering, "I'm glad you're here, Flynn. We have a lot to talk about."

I just nod because I'm not used to this. People don't smile at me. They try not to look at me at all and the only people who ever seem pleased to see me are my friends in Club Mafia. I've had women glance at me a different way sometimes, softer, with a deep yearning in their eyes, but this look is nothing like that. It's one I have yet to process in my mind and I'm struggling to understand how to deal with it.

We head to a room as described, decorated completely in blue and like every room I have seen so far, this one is light filled and chic, yet homey and welcoming. It's as if I'm in the Twilight Zone and have stepped inside a movie. This world isn't dark and formed with rough edges. Nothing bad can happen in a place like this and I'm doubtful anything ever has.

We take our seats at the polished mahogany table that is positioned beside a glass wall overlooking the garden.

The sun filters inside the room, touching my face with a warmth that relaxes me a little.

Vivian seems nervous and I can't blame her for that because I know I cut a menacing figure without even trying. In my defense, it's been crafted from years of pain and abuse and is the only shield I have in the cruel world I inhabit.

The door opens and I stand respectfully as a man heads inside and smiles with a curiosity I share.

Dimitri Sullivan is larger than life and every bit as commanding as his photograph. In fact, it doesn't do the man justice because he commands respect with just one glance. His eyes find his wife's and I see the concern in them and the look she shoots him tells me they are happy, which in turn makes me happy.

He moves across and offers me his hand and says in a deep voice, "Welcome..."

"Um, Flynn, sir."

As he crushes my hand in his powerful grip, I struggle to see any similarities to Massimo, his apparent brother. A vile creature of the most demented kind, and I kind of expected his brother would appear much the same. However, I am pleasantly surprised to find he is nothing like him and relax a little as he regards me through curious eyes.

"So, Flynn, you came here for answers I believe, you must have many questions."

He gestures to the seat behind me and as we all sit, I nod, swallowing the nerves and decide to get straight to the point. Something tells me he would appreciate that.

"Firstly, please accept my apologies for turning up unannounced. I suppose I thought you wouldn't agree to see me if I called ahead."

"Why not?"

Dimitri looks curious, and I shrug. "Forgive me, sir, but when people know where I come from, they do everything possible to avoid me."

Vivian shakes her head sadly and surprises me by saying wistfully, "Flynn, we all have a past and I'm not that proud of my own. It's what you do with the future that counts now."

Dimitri takes her hand and kisses it gently and just that one sweet gesture disarms me in an instant.

"Don't be ashamed of your beginnings, Flynn. Do you think it was easy for any of us? When I came to Seattle, I was running from a life I couldn't wait to get away from. Vivian was much the same and there will be no judging anyone here. So, tell us what you know."

"I'm sorry, sir, it's virtually nothing. I was raised by my uncle. At least that's the name I call him. I'm not even sure if we're related by blood at all. I hope not, anyway."

Vivian looks concerned. "What's his name?"

"Wesley Vasquez." Just the name causes the blood to drain from her face and Dimitri looks as if I just killed his cat.

"Does he know you're here?" Dimitri says with a sudden urgency, and I shake my head. "No. I thought it for the best."

The relief is almost tangible and Dimitri growls. "I fucking hate that man."

"You know him?"

I'm surprised at that, and he nods vigorously. "I grew up with the bastard haunting my dreams. He was my brother's best friend, and they made my life a misery."

Vivian looks as if she's about to hurl and I wonder about that as she grips Dimitri's hand tightly and appears to be having a panic attack.

"Are you ok?" I say with concern, and she nods, trying to smile as Mrs. Hedges enters the room carrying a silver tray laden with food.

Conversation stops as the food is delivered and only when she leaves does Vivian expel the breath she's holding and say sadly, "I worked for him."

I say nothing and she smiles ruefully. "My beginnings were hard, Flynn. My family hated the choices I made and cut me out of their lives. I found work in Wesley's club as a waitress and lived a life I'm not proud of."

She seems upset about that, and Dimitri places his arm around her shoulder and shakes his head. "You weren't to blame for what happened."

I sense I'm not going to like this conversation, judging by the expression on their faces, and Vivian flashes me a despairing glance that doesn't make me feel any better.

"You must be curious, Flynn, but can I ask you a question?"

"Of course."

I wonder what I can possibly tell her, and she whispers, "Did Wesley ever mention your father?"

I can see the whites of her knuckles as she grips hard on her cutlery and her anxious eyes tell me I'm not going to like what I hear. "He told me he was a punter. That you were a prostitute and never found out who he was. He also told me you sold me to him because you didn't want me."

Just saying the words cause my voice to shake and I hate laying it out there as her eyes fill with pain and Dimitri snaps, "Fucking bastard."

"It's ok, honey, I'm not surprised."

Vivian shakes her head and fixes me with a desolate glance that immediately makes me raise my guard.

"I'm sorry, Flynn, but I know who your father is, and it's not good."

The hairs on the back of my neck stand to attention and the pain in Dimitri's eyes tells me this is not going to sit well with me. Vivian looks down as if ashamed and whispers, "I was working at the club past closing time. Clearing the glasses and doing what I always did."

She looks up and smiles. "Contrary to what you were told, I wasn't a prostitute, just a waitress in a bar trying to earn my rent money. I was only twenty-one and struggling. I had no family, no friends and only a small apartment on the wrong side of town. I say apartment. It was one room in a block that was home to drug users and prostitutes. I had dreams, though. I wanted to make enough money to buy a bus ticket to a better place. Find a good neighborhood where I could settle and make an honest life for myself. I didn't want much, just to meet someone nice and settle down. Have a family and watch them grow.

She sighs heavily. "That night changed everything. It was when I was finishing up and went to get my coat that someone grabbed me from behind. They placed a hood over my head and tied it tight at the neck. I screamed, but I was punched hard and pulled roughly into a room. I felt my clothes fall away and then I was face down on a bed."

Her words paint a familiar scene that I have lived with all my life, and I already know what's coming as she sobs. "I was raped - repeatedly. I'm not even sure how long it went on for. It was brutal, despicable, and rough. I must have blacked out and woke to find my nightmare was still with me. I thought I would lose my life that night and prayed for it. I must have passed out again because when I woke up, I was tied to a bed and my legs shackled to the frame. I was sore, bruised and tasted blood in my mouth and remember how cold I was. I have never been so cold and then the door opened, and your uncle walked in and just laughed."

"It was him?" My voice is rough and filled with revenge as I watch the helpless tears slide down her face that she brushes angrily away. "Apparently not."

Dimitri's face is like thunder as she whispers, "He told me not to say a word about what happened if I wanted to live and that he was sorry and would make things right. I was confused, and he seemed almost gentle as he untied my legs and gave me a sweater to cover my battered body. He appeared upset, and it threw me a little and told me the man who had done this was sick. He wasn't the kind of man you reported to the cops and lived to make a statement. He would do what he could to compensate me for what happened and would make sure I had a place to live and money to get by."

"Did he give you a name?" The rage swirls inside me like a cyclone building and she nods sadly. "He told me it was Massimo Delauren."

I think my world ends with those two words. The darkness circles me and claws at my soul. It tears me apart and makes a mockery of everything I ever hoped for. Any other name would have been better than that one and the pain in Dimitri's eyes and the defeat on Vivian's face makes me so angry I could start a war on my own.

I am devastated.

I am crushed, bitter and defeated because that man's blood runs in my veins and marks me unclean. The madness in me is that deranged part of him, and the worst thing of all is that my greatest enemy is also my father.

It's too much to deal with and I'm unsure what to do. I'm used to taking off and dealing with my demons in the only way I can, but I'm in new territory. I am far away from everything familiar and floundering.

It's too much. I can't cope and as I dive headfirst into hell, an Angel reaches out and stops me from falling. A cool hand grasps mine and another one grabs my face and directs it to hers. I blink as Vivian looks at me with a hard expression in her eyes and says roughly, "Focus on me, Flynn and know you are better than him. His sin is not yours and you will prove to everyone you are better than he will ever be. Life may knock us down but it's how we get up that counts. Stand strong, Flynn and make *your* life count. Be magnificent because our past has no claim on our future. Let us help you. You are not alone. Not anymore. We've got you honey, and you have a future with us."

The words are ones I have been longing to hear my whole life and yet are the result of ones I *never* wanted to hear. I made my peace years ago with the fact I would never discover who my father was, and I wish that was still the case. I was created by a monster in a vile act of depravity and violence. I am the result of a traumatic experience and the chaos that swirls in my soul was put there by the biggest monster life created. I am part of that madness. I was grown from immorality, and I don't deserve to sit among these decent folk who are staring at me with compassion and an emotion I am finding hard to deal with.

The demons circle and destiny changes direction because my mission has been shot down in flames before I even got started. Marriage for power. That was the real reason I came here and there is no way in hell that can ever happen now because it turns out I'm family and the half-blood prince.

What the fuck am I going to do now?

CHAPTER 5

LOUISA

Somehow, I manage to read through the contract and make a few notes, but my thoughts are never far away from the stranger downstairs. Who is he and what's got my father so rattled?

That alone has me guessing because he never gets rattled. He's always in control and I'm shocked at seeing a different side to him.

Wearily, I change for dinner and pull on my usual shapeless sweater and leggings and run my fingers through my hair. I'm guessing as always, Sienna will be polished perfection. Usually while she waits for another admirer to come calling.

We are so different. She is everything I'm not and tell myself I don't want to be. A stunning blonde with pretty blue eyes and a stick thin figure that would be the envy of everyone, me included. No matter how hard I try, I can't shift the pounds and resign myself to a ruthless cycle of gluttony followed by starvation and a desperate yearning for acceptance. I've always been the ugly duckling of the family. My mom wasn't a great beauty and was my father's childhood sweetheart. They met at college, and he was nowhere near as successful as he became.

Mainly because of her. She was the brains with none of the beauty. Together they created an empire and then she was struck down by cancer in her prime, leaving him devastated and me without a mother.

I was too young to remember, and then he quickly met Crystal Monroe, Sienna's mother. Growing up as the ugly duckling in a family of swans was difficult, and I developed a hard shell. Crystal was a vain, needy woman who was not unkind, but her indifference hurt us both. Sienna craved a loving mother but was always made to feel as if she was in the way. I was happy to be disregarded but hated the way she played my father.

Endless arguments about countless affairs drove them apart and my father changed from a happy, loving man into a depressed, distrustful shell of himself. It was almost a relief when she ran off to Hollywood, telling Sienna she would send for her when she was set up. Sienna is still waiting, and it must hurt like hell.

Then he met Vivian, who was like a breath of fresh air through the family. A kind, loving woman who restored the smile on my father's face and gave us a home for once in our lives. She worked at my father's company as his assistant. Classic really, but they soon fell in love and now she heads up the home and creates a loving environment for him to return to every night. Vivian has always bent double to make us feel like one of her own daughters, and I know that Sienna is as grateful as I am about that.

Now things are set to change, and I wonder if our cozy bubble is about to burst, but nothing prepares for me for my first meeting with the stranger who came calling earlier on today.

I head into the dining room as is customary at seven o'clock every night. We dine as a family before disappearing off for the rest of the evening. I usually go to my room to read, and Sienna heads out on yet another date. Dad and Vivian watch tv, or accept one of the countless invitations they receive, but tonight we have a visitor and as soon as I enter the room, I guess immediately who he is.

Two dark eyes watch me approach, and it's as if he is reading my soul. Impenetrable, dark pools of mystery that take my breath away. It's difficult to see what color his hair is as he has bleached it blonde, and it sits slightly spiky on top of a devastatingly handsome face. The rough stubble decorating his jaw creates an element of danger as his beauty entrances me and draws me in, captivating my senses and taking my mind hostage. He is the most handsome man I have ever met and yet there's an edge of danger to him that makes my skin prickle with energy and causes a shiver to fizz my blood with the promise that things will never be the same again.

His dark suit is well cut and the black silk shirt unbuttoned low enough to reveal dark looking script, intrigues me. His fingers are adorned with huge silver rings that resemble weapons and the air of mystery surrounding him makes my libido fire up and take notes.

However, the most unmistakable thing about him is his resemblance to Vivian and it can only be because of one thing. This man is related to her, and I wonder what that means for us.

Before I can speak, Sienna pushes past me and stops dead in her tracks, her hand flying to her mouth to capture the low 'fuck' that rushes past her lips. The irritated expression on my father's face almost makes it amusing, but for once I'm in total agreement with my sister. Fuck indeed.

"Girls." Vivian steps forward, looking anxious.

"This is, um, well, this is, Flynn. My son."

I stare at her in shocked surprise and note the flush to her skin and the anxiety in her eyes.

Sienna gasps, "Wow, now you say it, it's pretty obvious. I mean, Vivian, he's the image of you."

I detect a hint of pride in his eyes as he hears her words, but it's the look he's casting in my direction that floors me a little. Those eyes are probing into me as if he wants answers I don't have, and I shake myself and force a welcoming smile on my face.

"I'm pleased to meet you." I smile shyly and get an amused grin in return as Sienna steps in front of me and offers him her hand. "Likewise, I'm sure. I'm Sienna, daughter number two. Wow, I can't believe this. Where have you been all my life?"

My father rolls his eyes, and the stranger merely smiles politely. "I'm pleased to meet you, Sienna."

He looks past her to me, and I could drown in the deep pools of darkness that glitter with danger and something sparks between us that flusters me. He holds out his hand and I grab it quickly, pumping furiously and saying quickly, "Um, Louisa. I'm pleased to meet you."

His fingers wrap around mine, and a huge wave of delirium engulfs me as I long for him to tug me closer and weave those fingers around my heart. Then everything changes as Vivian says quickly, "Flynn is family. I mean, well, I don't know how to say this…"

I'm surprised because she's uncomfortable about something and appears lost for words and my father steps forward and takes her hand. "What Vivian means is that Flynn is also my nephew and, well, your cousin, girls."

I stare at him sharply because what the fuck is going on? Sienna looks troubled. "I don't understand."

I risk a glance at Flynn and see the storm brewing in his eyes and imagine an icy hand clutching my heart strings. Something about this is bad and Vivian says almost shame faced, "Flynn's father is your dad's brother, your Uncle Massimo."

Sienna appears as shocked as I am, and it doesn't appear that anyone is happy about that. For some reason, I am devastated, and I don't understand why. Flynn looks sick and Vivian looks as if she's about to cry and the murderous rage in my father's eyes makes for a very awkward moment.

Pushing down my disappointment, I smile and say kindly, "Then welcome to the family, Flynn. We should drink to that."

I'm guessing everyone could use a stiff one and my father says quickly, "Of course, this is a happy occasion, after all. Champagne is needed, and lots of it."

As he heads off, I watch Vivian struggling with her composure, and feel sorry for her. Smiling at Flynn, I move toward my stepmother and hug her warmly. "Congratulations, Vivian. You must be so happy he's here."

The bright tears in her eyes expresses her gratitude and she smiles. "I am."

I turn to Flynn and am quietly unsettled by the expression in his eyes, and I swallow the lump in my throat as I smile. "I hope you're going to stick around for a while. It will be good to get to know you."

He nods, looking a little out of place, and I watch as Sienna grabs his hand and says with excitement, "I could show you how things work around here. Parade you around town and you can hang out with me and my friends."

"I don't think…" I interrupt because, from the horror on his face, Flynn would rather stab his own eyes out and she rounds on me furiously. "At least I have friends, Louisa. What would you do to make him welcome? Read him a chapter from one of your romance books? No, leave it with me. I'll show Flynn how it works around here, and it can begin tonight."

She turns and says with excitement. "There's a party at my friend's house. You could come with me, and I'll introduce you to everyone."

I roll my eyes behind her back, causing him to smile a little and luckily Vivian steps in and says evenly, "Perhaps another night honey. Flynn has just got here and I'm keen to catch up. It was such a sweet thought, though."

Sienna nods and looks a little disappointed but cheers up when she takes the seat beside him at dinner. I am seated opposite him and am conscious the entire time of those dark eyes staring at me with a curiosity I can't explain.

As we take our first family meal together, you could cut the atmosphere with a knife. It's awkward as fuck, yet the most exciting night I have ever spent.

CHAPTER 6

FLYNN

My emotions are in overload, and for a man who usually has none, I am struggling. To meet my mother and learn the terrible truth of my birth in one day is more than I can cope with. Then I met her. Louisa Sullivan. The woman I came here for who is everything I imagined she would be and more.

But everything changed when my father's name spilled from my mother's lips. Destiny shifted on the track and sent me down a new one. It doesn't help that I wish I was on the old one. Seducing Louisa would be a pleasure because she is everything I love in a woman. Wild, unpolished, and innocent. No mask to hide behind and an endearing uncertainty as she faces life head on and struggles with that. I know everything about this woman, more than she even knows about herself, because that is how I earned my nickname. The Angel. I thrive on educating women like her in how good it is to be loved. Giving them a moment of their own when they experience the power of desire. Building them up and showing them how powerful they can be.

When I learned there were two daughters and saw their

images on the screen, I knew who I wanted. Not the polished, perfect one who finds life easy. The other one. The one who lives in the shadows and believes she's not good enough. I want her and fate, like the cruellest bitch, has snatched her away and left me floundering. Which way do I turn and what will it mean for Club Mafia?

Sienna chatters through dinner without gasping for air and I suppose it's a good thing because her parents are struggling with the situation just as much as I am. They didn't expect this. They probably didn't want this, and yet the expression in Vivian's eyes when she first set eyes on me will stay with me forever. It was a mother's unconditional love for a child. Her dead baby grew into a man and came to find her. I will never forget that, and I will never do anything to hurt her. My father —well, that's another story entirely.

By the time the meal ends, Sienna stands and says with a sigh, "I should go. Harrison is outside."

"Then he can come and collect you like a gentleman."

Dimitri's low growl makes me smirk inside because it's obvious he's very protective of his daughters, which in my opinion, is a very good thing. Sienna obviously doesn't agree because she huffs and rolls her eyes, saying over her shoulder, "God, this is so embarrassing."

As she heads out of the room, Vivian smiles adoringly at her husband. "Go easy on him, darling. He's a good kid."

I catch the expression on Louisa's face, which tells me she knows something they don't, and I know the type he is in an instant.

They soon return and Harrison enters, looking like the typical prep bastard he is. Floppy hair greased to one side and the smug smile of a man who has never had to work hard at anything. His white shirt is dressed with a sweater tied around his neck and his chinos hang low on his hips as he smirks around the room.

"Sir, ma'am, good evening."

He nods with respect and then casts a curious inquisitive stare at me, not even acknowledging Louisa is in the room at all. My eyes narrow as I peer at him with dark consideration and Harrison is either high already, or stupid because he doesn't seem to notice the sudden tension.

"I promise to look after your girl, sir. No drinking and I'll make sure she's home by midnight."

He stares fondly at Sienna, who bats her fake lashes and rests a false painted fingernail on his arm, giggling with adoration as she gazes up at his ridiculous over-inflated ego.

"I'll hold you to that, son."

Her father stares him down and I can tell he hates Harrison but knows this is Sienna's world. Her type thrives on running with the popular crowd and would die rather than not be considered the queen of all she surveys.

He offers her his arm and as she giggles stupidly, they turn and leave the room, followed by an exasperated sigh from her father.

"Fuck me, I need a drink."

Vivian sighs. "I wish she would open her eyes and see the full picture. What are we going to do with that girl?"

I steal a glance at Louisa, who catches my eye and grins before turning to her father and saying with a smile. "I should leave you all to talk. I'll be in my room."

"Actually, Louisa…" Vivian says quickly, "I'm sorry to ask, but your father and I have a drinks engagement at City Hall tonight."

She turns to me and says apologetically. "I'm so sorry to leave you on your first night and if we could cancel, I would in a heartbeat."

"It's fine, I understand." I smile to reassure her, and she nods, looking a little agitated before turning to Louisa.

"Please, can I ask you to show Flynn to the guest room and around the house? Make sure he has everything he needs."

Louisa nods as Vivian turns to me and says with concern, "I promise we will spend tomorrow together."

I can tell she feels bad about leaving and yet I'm keen to spend time with the woman who has taken my interest in a surprising way.

"It's fine. I completely understand, and we can catch up tomorrow."

Dimitri says with a sigh. "I have meetings tomorrow, but we'll talk when I get home. We have much to discuss."

My first impression of Dimitri Sullivan is a good one. If anything, I admire him more than I thought I would because I can tell he has a deep love for his family and a burning hatred for his brother. It was evident in his eyes when he heard his name and those are qualities we share. Maybe I can use that to my advantage and bring power to Club Mafia in a different way. Family power by birth right is every bit as powerful as by marriage.

One thing's certain, my mission hasn't changed. If anything, the need has only intensified and bringing Massimo Delauren down is now my only goal in life and I will make him pay for every sin he has committed and even the ones he has yet to make happen.

CHAPTER 7

LOUISA

This is an interesting situation I never saw coming. Alone with what could be my cousin and yet somehow, I wish things were very different.

Not because I don't like Flynn, hell I don't even know him, but what I've seen so far is favorable.

No, it's the feeling deep inside when he looks at me with those sexy, dangerous eyes. No man has ever looked at me like that and it's just my luck that I'm related to the first one who does.

Vivian and my father leave the room and it's a little awkward for all of a second.

I'm surprised when Flynn flashes me a blinding smile that puts me at ease immediately.

"Sorry you've got to babysit. I'll try to make it a painless experience."

"It's fine, really."

I regard him with interest, but not enough to make it obvious and laugh a little awkwardly.

"So, the guided tour. I'm guessing you're here to stay for a while, so you'll need the extended one."

He looks a little sad and I wonder if I've said anything wrong and he sighs. "I hope I can stay, but well, I have a life in LA that's calling me back."

He holds up his phone and shows me the number of notifications on the screen, and he sighs. "I can ignore them to a point before it gets more difficult."

"Tell me about your life, Flynn." I say impulsively and he replies wearily, "You wouldn't want to know."

"You're wrong."

He raises his eyes and I smile shyly. "I would. I mean, what do you do for a job? Have you a family now, a girl perhaps?"

I color up as I say it and hate how transparent I am, and he smiles with amusement. "I have no one, Louisa. Just a group of friends who care, but nobody else."

"That's…"

"Sad." He sighs. "It's not good, but I have never known any different."

I smile nervously and nod toward the door.

"Shall we start our tour?"

"After you."

He stands to the side, and my heart flutters at the look in his eye. I'm guessing it's because I'm inexperienced in these things and read more into it than there is, but I could swear he is flirting with me. It's the lazy way he drags his eyes across my body, looking as if he approves of what he sees. I've never had that. Nobody ever gazes at me with interest, merely disbelief that I'm Sienna's sister. Wishing like crazy I had worn something different, part of me is shouting at me, no screaming at me that this is one forbidden obsession because he is my cousin, for Christ's sake.

Quickly, I remind us both and say a little hesitantly, "Do you know Massimo Delauren?"

"Not personally. Do you?"

"No, but I've heard of him."

"He's your uncle. I'm sure that you have."

"It's not good, I'm afraid."

"It never is when his name is mentioned."

"How does it feel knowing he's…"

I hesitate because I'm not sure we should be having this conversation and Flynn appears angry as he says sharply, "Like someone has ripped out my heart and burned it with acid."

"I see." I'm a little taken aback by the anger in his voice and he sighs, before placing his hand on my arm to stop me.

"I'm sorry, Louisa. Today has been a learning curve I never expected. I should concentrate on the good that came out of it and focus on Vivian. Tell me about her."

Just his hand on me has distracted me a little and for a moment I hesitate and say awkwardly, "Um, she's great. I love her like a mother and have nothing bad to say about her."

"That's good to hear."

He smiles and I can't stop staring because I have never seen a man who blinds me as much as he does. It's like staring into the sun and being momentarily dazzled by the intensity of its rays. I am experiencing an attraction I can't reason with, and like a lovesick puppy, I have placed him high on a pedestal and already idolize him. I must be delirious because he is paying me attention and so I drag my eyes away and say in a higher voice than usual, "This is the games room."

I lead him into a place my father adores. A typical men's retreat with a pool table, a mahogany bar, and a huge television, around which are comfortable chairs and low-slung tables.

"Impressive." Flynn appears fascinated as he gazes around the room, and I say quickly. "What's your home like, Flynn?"

I wonder if he lives in a similar house, and he laughs with an edge of derision. "It's big, bold, and distasteful. Filled with antiques and dusty tapestries, hidden doors and secretive passageways, all leading to the most uncomfortable rooms anyone would hate to explore. It's guarded like a fortress and hides many sins. It's hell on earth and I pray you never witness it first-hand."

"Oh."

I don't know what else to say, and he laughs darkly. "This is a home, Louisa. Mine is a prison. I was brought up there by my uncle, who made it his mission in life to make mine hell on earth. The only person who ever showed me affection was my nanny, Rosemary."

He breaks off and looks away, and I can tell the memory is not a pleasant one.

"What happened? To Rosemary, I mean."

I wish I hadn't asked, because it's as if the shutters open for the briefest moment and I witness a festering wound behind his eyes. Rage, grief and hatred flash in a cocktail of misery and I almost think it will bring him down, but he closes his eyes and when he opens them, the fire has gone.

He says coldly, "She died."

I open my mouth with more questions that are immediately forgotten as he fixes his attention on me and says huskily, "What about you? Tell me about Louisa."

"Me?"

Nobody ever asks me about me and for good reason. There is absolutely nothing to say and so I laugh nervously.

"I'm not interesting enough to have a story to tell, Flynn. I have no friends; my sister doesn't understand me, and I spend all my time studying and trying to be as good at business as my father."

"I don't believe that."

"What?"

"That you have no friends and I find you very interesting as it happens."

"You do."

I must appear shocked at that, and he surprises me by moving behind the bar and grabbing two glasses.

"Do you think your father would mind if we had a couple of drinks and shot some pool?"

"I guess not." I'm surprised and a little nervous, saying, "To be honest, I don't drink, and I've never played pool."

He must wonder what planet I'm from and yet all he does is smile sweetly. "OK, two firsts coming up. Let me educate you."

I perch on a bar stool and watch him make two drinks.

"What are they?"

I'm interested to find out, and he grins. "Vodka Martinis."

"Vodka, I'm not sure…"

"Trust me, you'll love them."

He slides one across and leans on the bar, raising his own glass to mind and I swallow hard because this man is doing something to me inside that I never saw coming.

"To family and new beginnings."

"To family." I'm sure my voice must be dressed in disappointment because he winks and sips the drink, watching me through those dark, disturbing eyes the entire time.

As I hold the glass to my lips, I must wince as the bitter liquid coats my tongue and he whispers, "You'll get used to it."

Trying so hard not to be a complete buzz kill, I take a swig and almost choke on the fumes.

"People like that." I stare at him in shock, and he laughs softly. "As I said, you'll get used to it. There are many things in life that start off disgusting, but you soon develop an urgent need for."

Once again, he winks and fuck me, I'm flooding with heat right now and without thinking, I almost down the drink in one, loving the burn as it douses the fire inside with even more gasoline.

Flynn turns to the pool table and removes two cues from the rack on the wall and hands one to me.

"Let me teach you."

"OK."

I stand awkwardly as he sets it up and explains what he's doing every step of the way. Perhaps it's the drink, or it's probably him, but I can't rip my eyes from his body as he shrugs off his jacket and rolls up his sleeves. I stare at the intricate ink on his forearms and am strangely turned on by that. In fact, I'm a raging mass of hormones right now and once again, wish like crazy I had never thought a sweater was a good outfit choice for dinner.

As he calls me forward to take my turn, I almost hyperventilate when he stands behind me and positions his arms around my shoulders and demonstrates how to hold the cue properly. My mind is buzzing, my lady parts are throbbing, and I don't think I have long before my heart gives out on me. Yet throughout my embarrassing body meltdown, Flynn speaks huskily in my ear as he explains the game, and I swear I am in heaven.

CHAPTER 8

FLYNN

I should be tossed out with the trash for the wicked thoughts running through my head right now. I couldn't help myself. I had to have one touch. One sniff of a woman who is blinding me to what's right and wrong. She is wrong, so wrong on a whole different level, but there's an aching need to feel her in my arms. I am going to Hell, and you know what? It's worth it.

There has been something pounding in my head since my mother's revelation that doesn't sit right with me. As the shock subsided, the questions reared their heads and now I've had time to process the information, I'm not so sure anymore.

As Louisa struggles to maintain control of her cue, I stand back and smile at her efforts. She's so determined to succeed at this, and I'm guessing she's a girl who doesn't like to give up. We share that in common and as she misses yet another shot and curses, I head back to the bar. "Fancy another."

"Is that a good idea?" Her eyes are wide, but from the flush to her cheeks and the brightness in her eyes, I can tell she's relishing every minute of this.

"One more won't hurt."

I wink and love how she blushes adorably and as she perches on the stool and stares at me with undisguised longing, I can already tell she feels the same.

"There's something bugging me, Louisa. Would you mind if I ran it past you?"

I fix the drinks and catch her eye and she seems surprised at being asked. "Of course, I'll help with anything."

Sighing, I slide the cocktail across the bar and fix her with a desperate look.

"I am struggling to comprehend that Massimo is my father."

"Why?"

She looks interested, and I shrug. "You see, I get my uncle, more than anyone, and what Vivian told me doesn't add up. In fact, I would believe it more if he were my father. It's something he would do."

"That's terrible." She looks sick and I say roughly, "He is despicable and not a very nice man."

"So, what are you thinking?"

Her eyes are bright, and nobody has ever looked so beautiful to me as she does, cast in the glow of the lamplight with the soft flush to her cheeks caused by alcohol and dangerous living. For her, anyway.

"Why would my uncle help Vivian? It doesn't make sense. I have never known him to help anyone before. It doesn't add up. Then there's the part where she was told I had died at birth. Who told her that? What happened that day?"

I sigh. "I have so many questions and for some reason, I'm guessing my uncle has the answers. Vivian only knows what he told her, which is probably only what he wants her to know. Then there's Massimo."

I break off and hate the sound of his name on my lips. "If I was his son, why have I never met him? He's my uncle's friend. Wouldn't he be curious?"

"Perhaps he doesn't know."

Louisa's soft voice makes me stop and for a moment there is silence as we both think about the problem.

"Maybe your uncle never told him and, for his own reasons, decided to raise you as his. Possibly it's because..."

"I am his."

The brutal truth hits me a second time and I wonder how I got so lucky. Two potential sperm donors, and both are as rotten as hell. Lucky me.

"So, how can we discover the truth?"

Her voice is husky and laced in need, and I wish I could show her how sexy I'm finding that right now. Instead I smile ruefully.

"I guess I start looking."

I don't miss the fact she said we and I am letting her down gently. This is my war, and I am not dragging her into battle with me. It's obvious she doesn't miss the subtle correction and I love how her eyes flash as she says with a slight slur to her voice, "*We*, Flynn. You're not on your own anymore. We could be related, then again, possibly not so I have a vested interest in helping you discover the truth."

"Is that right?"

"Yes. It is and I could help you. I know people."

It amuses me to see the raw passion flashing in her eyes and I say with a smile, "What people?"

My question surprises her and makes her pause for a moment before she blushes and shrugs, "Just people. So, this is what we'll do."

She stands and starts pacing the room, and I swear I can't tear my eyes away from the most magnificent sight. Beautiful long brown wavy hair that shines as if it's been waxed. Full, plump hips that sway sexily as she walks, her sweater rising against the curve of her ass. Her astonishing green eyes flash as she contemplates the problem and the wet ruby red lips that are as natural as the day she was born beg for my attention.

Just the swell of her breasts as they dance under her sweater causes my cock serious discomfort right now and just imagining experiencing that soft flesh, flush against my skin, makes me almost weep at fate for being such a bitch.

I want her. I crave her and I can't do anything about that all the time we're fucking related and so it's for my own sanity I need to discover the truth because if I'm not related to this goddess, I'm making her my wife whether she likes it or not.

Despite the fact I'm enjoying spending cozy time with Louisa, I'm not sure her parents would appreciate me corrupting their daughter as soon as I arrive, so I say with a smile, "Perhaps we should grab a coffee. You haven't shown me the kitchen yet."

"Of course. Follow me."

She appears a little unsteady and I grab her arm to help her along and she giggles. "I think I might be allergic to Martinis."

Biting back a grin, I help her along the hallway, and she directs me to a huge kitchen that spans the length of the house. "Let me make the drinks this time."

Once again, she slurs a little and I can't help noticing how adorable she is. So natural and unaware of how she is affecting me, and I wonder why nobody else sees what I do. They are so intent on the polish and façade, they don't stare deeper than that. There is so much more beneath the surface of girls who have more on their minds than their appearance. A virtual world of delight and I'm the lucky bastard spending time with this one.

This time I watch from the bar stool as she shovels coffee into the filter and pours in the water. As she removes two mugs from the cupboard she sighs.

"You know, Flynn, we've only just met and yet this is the most fun I've had in well, probably ever. Do you pity me because I do?"

She giggles and I physically ache for one taste of her, but

instead, I smile. "I'm having fun too. So, what do you do for pleasure around here?"

"I read." She sighs wistfully. "Sienna likes to party. She has a huge group of friends and is out most nights."

"You don't want to join in?"

"No. Every time I go with her, I end up calling a cab home. I don't fit in with her world and I'm guessing never will."

"What about your own friends? You must have some."

"I do, but they moved away, many to work and others to do relief work abroad."

"They sound cool."

"Not really." She laughs out loud. "Cool is the wrong choice of words in the normal sense, but to me, they are."

She regards me through her insanely long lashes. "Tell me about your friends."

"It's best you don't ask." I laugh out loud because introducing Louisa to my fellow club members would be like a sleepover at Hansel and Gretel's gingerbread cottage.

She yawns and I note it's barely nine, and she says with a deep sigh, "I'm sorry. I'm such a lightweight I'm usually in bed by now, reading."

"Then you should show me to my room and turn in for the night."

"You wouldn't mind?'

"No. It's been a demanding day already."

"Do you have any bags?" She looks worried about that, and I shake my head. "No. To be honest, I never thought this through. It's good though. I'll pick up some stuff in the morning."

"It's ok, we have some supplies you could use. Follow me."

She grabs her coffee and I follow her, surprised at how different this is to what I expected.

We pass through stunning decorated hallways that offer a

glimpse of chic elegance through partially open doors and it's as if the house is decorated in good vibes. I like it and I like my new family. My only concern is that I like one of them a little too much.

CHAPTER 9

LOUISA

I direct Flynn to the guest room and the walk back to mine is a confusing one. Just leaving him there was strange. Wrong even. I enjoyed our time together and when he mentioned his doubts about his father, I seized on it as if a lifeline was thrown in my direction. Is it possible? Did his uncle lie to Vivian? Flynn certainly believes it's a possibility and so rather than grab my novel from the bookstand, I seize my laptop and start googling the hell out of Massimo Delauren.

It sobers me up pretty quickly, and I stare in amazement at the lifestyle of a man who appears shrouded in secrecy. Nothing but rumor and gossip about a man who appears to live way beyond even my father's means, and I wonder about him. I cross reference my own family history and am surprised when my father isn't mentioned on the same page. It's as if all traces of their parentage have been erased and it's not evident that they are related at all.

As I glance at my phone, I wonder if I have the courage to make the call I'm considering because I wasn't kidding when I told Flynn I knew people. I do. Very influential ones who would be able to find what I need with no questions asked, but

I will risk my father finding out I've been snooping. He might be angry about involving others in family business when he still needs to come to terms with it himself.

The trouble is, I've always been impetuous, and I can't possibly sleep with this weighing heavily on my mind.

Tossing caution aside, I reach for my phone and press call and hope like crazy he doesn't answer.

"Louisa mi angel."

"Uncle Pedro, I'm sorry to call so late."

"It's never too late to call me. Are you in trouble?"

He sounds anxious and I experience a surge of love for my godfather.

"No, but I wondered if you could tell me anything about dad's brother, Massimo."

"I could, but the question is, why are you asking?"

"For a friend."

"And this friend, does he or she have a name?"

Now I'm not so sure this was such a good idea. I don't want to get Flynn in any trouble, and I certainly don't want to upset my father, so I backtrack quickly.

"It's ok, I shouldn't have asked. I'll ask dad when he comes home."

"Ok mi querido but if he doesn't answer your questions, you get back in touch. Say hi to your parents."

"Thanks uncle, sleep well."

His low laughter makes me smile.

"I always do querido, it's the rest who don't."

I cut the call and feel so stupid. What did that achieve but alert him to a problem that I'm pretty sure he's on the phone with my father about now?

I don't know what I expected, but I thought he'd give me something, at least.

Once again, I turn to the web and as I look at a grainy picture of my absent uncle Massimo, I peer closer to see if there is any resemblance to Flynn at all. If anything, the man gives me the creeps, and it's doubtful my sleep won't be filled with nightmares tonight.

I pray to God for Flynn's sake that this man isn't his father, and my mind returns to the whispered conversations I've overheard in the past concerning him.

It's obvious my father hates him, and it goes way back since before I was born. But how does Vivian know him, and how did she come to work at my father's office all the way from LA? There's obviously more to it, and I try to close my eyes on the frustration and banish the demons.

The trouble is, *he's* standing behind them. Flynn. I can't shake his image because I have an unhealthy interest in him. The looks he gave me, the gentle touch, and the concern in his eyes. That body that looked so powerful when he rolled up his sleeves and the smirk on his lips as he watched me drink his martini. The heat tears through me as I picture a different use of his lips.

Reaching under my sweater, I trace my fingers over the parts of me I wish he would kiss with his lips. I close my eyes and picture him beside me, sliding between my legs and doing something no man has ever done before. The wet heat reminds me how wicked I am because I haven't forgotten he could be family and that only makes it more forbidden, incestuous even and yet how can I switch this man off from my mind? I am shocked by my reaction to him and the fact he's from a mafia family only thrills me even more. He's dangerous in every way and as bad boys go, I have fixated on a good one because if God grants me only one wish in life, it's that Flynn is not connected to me by blood in the slightest.

* * *

My alarm wakes me at six am and bleary eyed, I stare at the ceiling. My mind struggles to catch up as I remember the events from yesterday. So much happened and I wonder what today will bring.

The trouble is, I don't have time to think about that because I have a meeting to attend, and I need to be focused because this is my future. It's so important for me to impress my father and prove I'm a worthy successor.

As I shower, my mind wanders back to Flynn, and I wonder if he slept well last night. Will I see him today and how long will he stay?

As I soap my body, it hums with a need for something that can never be mine and, as the frustration hits me, I force myself to concentrate on something else. Anything else, even my sister, because I can't allow myself to dream the impossible.

* * *

I head to breakfast and am not surprised that it's just my father and me and as I take my seat opposite him, he looks at me sharply.

"I had a call last night."

My heart sinks like a stone tossed in a river.

"I figured you might."

"What did you need to know?"

My father appears concerned, and I sigh. "I feel bad for Flynn. He was so cut up thinking Massimo is his father and wondered if his uncle had told Vivian the truth. He is doubtful about that, so I asked Uncle Pedro for help to see if he could tell me anything."

"There is nothing you need to know about that man."

"I'm not a child, dad." I huff impatiently. "I know he's your brother, and you fell out."

"Then you know everything I want you to."

He turns his attention to the newspaper, and I sigh with frustration.

A movement by the door diverts my attention and my heart lifts when Flynn enters the room and hesitates. "I'm sorry. I hope I'm not disturbing you."

I feel bad for him and smile my encouragement and as my father looks up, I watch a thousand emotions cross his face as he says kindly, "Take a seat, Flynn. Perhaps we should have that conversation now."

I look at him in surprise and he smiles. "You're right, Louisa. There are things that need to be said, and it's wrong of me to shut them down."

I'm more surprised at that than anything so far and a surge of love for my father hits me. He's such a decent man and I couldn't love him more than I do at this moment.

I catch Flynn's eye and smile reassuringly and don't miss the caginess in his own expression.

As I pour him a coffee I wave to the spare seat beside me and as he takes it, I settle down to listen to a story I am desperate to learn has a happy ending.

CHAPTER 10

FLYNN

It feels so wrong being here. Sleeping in an unfamiliar house while dodging my uncle's calls and hoping for answers that satisfy my own agenda. Most of all, I hate the possibility that Massimo Delauren is my father, and I may as well end my life now if that turns out to be true.

I hate him with such a passion it surprises me. The fact he took Winter and made her his wife from under our noses still rattles me now. It's become the most important thing in all our lives to bring her back to us. Angelo's sister, his twin, and my friend.

We failed in protecting her and now she lives with the biggest monster inside an impenetrable fortress. She appears happy in public, but there's a dead expression in her eyes that has no business being there. It's become so important to set her free I will stop at nothing to make it happen. Even if it means killing the man who is possibly my father. I would do it in a heartbeat for Winter, for Angelo and for Alessandro because that man is in torment, and I can't bear to comprehend what demons he lives with every day.

I know they were close. Something must have happened

between them, or he wouldn't have been affected so hard. No, I need to play my part in this and do what I can to end this monster's reign, so I stare at his brother in the hope he tells me something I can use to bring him down.

"Vivian told me you mentioned Iris Young, and I'm curious about that."

I sit up and take note because I'm still none the wiser of who she is and her involvement in my life, so I shrug and say firmly, "I was told to find Vivian Clark and Iris Young. Apparently, they would set me free, whatever that means."

Dimitri looks thoughtful and Louisa is concentrating hard and just the fact she's chewing on her lip with a nervous habit makes me long to see what they taste like for myself. I am now officially heading to hell.

"Iris Young was our governess when we were growing up." Dimitri says with no emotion in his voice.

I wasn't expecting that and can tell Louisa didn't either. "She was a formidable woman and Massimo in particular was scared to death of her." He chuckles as if that amuses him, and I can't believe for one second the great Massimo Delauren was afraid of an old woman.

Dimitri looks lost in the past as he revisits old wounds. "She was a tyrant. It was hard to be around her, but Massimo idolized her. It was evident in his eyes, and he did everything possible to make her proud of him. She never was. She was a vile woman who got off on tormenting us and when I headed off to school, I was just glad to be shot of them both."

He shakes his head. "Massimo is a year younger than me and had to tolerate her undivided attention. I'm not sure what happened to her when he was shipped off to school but I believe she found work with another family and that's the last I heard of her until you came calling, Flynn, so if you are looking for answers, I would advise you to start searching for her."

"Can we help?" Louisa speaks up and smiles sweetly across

the table at me. "I mean, can we help Flynn find her? It may be easier for us."

Dimitri nods. "I'll look into it. Leave it with me."

He stares at me sharply. "Louisa told me you had doubts about what your uncle told Vivian."

"I do."

He leans back in his seat and sighs.

"I'm not going to lie; I thought the same. Vivian never questioned it, but it doesn't sound like Massimo. For all his faults, he's not a rapist. Well, women, anyway."

Louisa looks up in shock and Dimitri checks himself as he realizes she's still here.

"Like I said, darling." He smiles sadly. "There's a reason I distanced myself from my brother, and his psychotic tendencies were just one of them."

"Oh, I'm sorry I'm late. Please forgive me."

Vivian heads into the room and my heart lifts. Quickly, I jump up and am surprised when she pulls me in for a hug and whispers, 'I'm so glad you're here, Flynn. We have so much to catch up on."

Like a breath of fresh air, she blasts through the room and expels the desolation our conversation has created. Dimitri smiles at her fondly and Louisa's face lights up. I am starting to realize my mother is a special woman, which makes what happened to her even harder to bear. She must have been destroyed, and the anger claws at my heart as I plot the cruelest of passings for whoever did that to her.

Another voice joins the conversation when Sienna enters the room.

"Oh, am I last? Sorry, I couldn't decide what to wear."

Louisa rolls her eyes because Sienna is wearing a pale pink dress that leaves nothing to the imagination and her perfectly made-up face pouts in my direction.

"Hey Flynn, you should tag along with me this afternoon.

Chloe Barton is having a pool party, and you would be most welcome."

I almost laugh out loud at the image of me at some posh kids' pool party and Louisa rolls her eyes. "I don't think…"

Sienna snaps, "What do you know, Louisa? You're a fun sponge, anyway. I mean, when was the last time you went to a pool party, huh? Actually, you should come too. Ashton Michaels will be there, and you should try to get him interested again."

My senses are prickling because whoever this guy is, I want to kill him with my bare hands and Louisa sighs with annoyance. "I told you, I'm not interested. He's so boring and has no conversation."

"Boring, that's rich, coming from the queen of boredom."

"That's enough, Sienna, apologize to your sister."

Dimitri growls and Sienna shrugs, not looking the least bit sorry as she snaps, "Soz, babe. Anyway, Flynn, do say you'll come. I was telling the gang about you last night and they are desperate for a glimpse. You'll make me the envy of everyone if you come."

I watch Louisa's face fall and hate the effect her sister has on her and I shake my head. "I'm sorry. Thanks for the invitation, but I have business to attend to."

"You do?" Vivian looks surprised, and I nod. "I need to clear my mind of a few things and could use the time to carry out some research."

Sienna yawns loudly. "Well, if you change your mind, you know where I am."

As she helps herself to a pastry, it's as if I've dodged a bullet. The thought of mixing with her friends leaves me cold, but her sister is another pleasure entirely.

Dimitri sighs heavily and looks at Louisa. "We should go. The meeting is at nine and I have some work to do beforehand."

I look up in surprise and note the smart dress Louisa is wearing that hugs her curves in all the right places. She has tied her hair back and her eyes shine with excitement as she stands.

Vivian looks surprised. "Oh, I forgot about your meeting. Will it take all day?"

Dimitri smiles and bends down, kissing his wife's cheek. "Only part of the morning. Come and meet me for lunch if you like."

"I'll let you know." Vivian looks in my direction and I say quickly, "It's fine. I really do have things to do."

As the family head off to their daily lives, it only reinforces how different my own is. There are no family breakfasts where we discuss our days. No messing around and no concern over how we're feeling. It's just business. Painful business that strips a man's soul and renders him a monster.

Just imagining the expression of horror on their faces if they see what I'm capable of fills me with sadness and as I glance up, I see Louisa staring at me with concern. She smiles briefly and for some reason it lifts my spirits because out of nowhere, this girl has managed to crawl inside my heart and let a little light in. With her I'm not on my own and I wonder about that. Could I have found someone to share my life with and will it be as a family rather than the lovers I would prefer?

If Massimo isn't my father, there is nothing stopping me from pursuing my original plan, which is why it's suddenly the most important thing in the world to find out once and for all who the fuck my father is.

CHAPTER 11

LOUISA

I'm strangely nervous. This is my first meeting, and I am so anxious to impress my father. It's common knowledge he wants to scale down his role at the company, and I've been working hard to become a worthy successor.

I even passed on university to start at the bottom of his empire and work my way up. I'm aware I'm riding a gold-lined elevator to the top, and this internship is not open to anyone but blood, but despite that, I've tried so hard to prove myself and now I'm attending my first ever meeting by his side. To say this day is monumental is an understatement.

Perhaps I shouldn't have drunk two martinis and spent half the night googling Massimo Delauren. I'm a little rough around the edges and my mind is filled with a certain visitor who has caught me off-guard.

Maybe today is just what I need to get things back on track and as we enter the building, I walk with a different spring in my step as I sense change is in the air.

My father sweeps through the building like the chief executive he is, and the awe and reverence on his employees' faces is well deserved. He's a good employer and a fair boss. He pays well and rewards his staff with parties and incentives if they achieve their goals. I want to be exactly like him and so as I sit at my place at the mahogany boardroom table, I remove my notebook and pen and vow to make every second count of this opportunity.

I'm not even sure what this meeting's about and as I wait, I spin in my chair and gaze out on the city below. It's a view I'm so familiar with, and I wonder if I will get to enjoy it as long as my father has. He built up his technology empire from one office to several across the country and, with my mother's help, they made billions.

Technology moved on fast, and they reaped the rewards. Being one of the main beneficiaries of that, I am keen to earn my place at his table. Which is why I'm a little unnerved at the current distraction consuming my thoughts, because when did I fixate on a man? Only him. Flynn Vasquez, possibly my cousin, possibly not. My thoughts turn to him, and I wonder what he's doing now. Business, he said. I'm not sure his idea of business is the same as ours and I can only imagine the horrors of his life as he struggles to get by.

The door opening interrupts my thoughts and I'm surprised to see a strange face enter and smile. "You must be Louisa Sullivan. I'm Brad Turner. I understand we will be working together."

"We will?"

I'm surprised because this is the first I've heard of him and before I can recover my father breezes in and says loudly, "Ah, I see you two have met already. Good to see you, Brad."

My father shakes his hand warmly before taking his seat at the head of the table and fixes us both with a firm expression.

"So, I should make some introductions. Louisa is my daughter and has been learning this business for many years, although only full time for the past two."

I'm not sure why, but I'm anticipating a meeting different

from the one I thought I'd be attending, and I nod, trying to grab control of my emotions.

My father points to Brad. "Brad has been working his way up in my Washington office. He's proven his worth and secured a great deal of business for Technofad. You could learn a lot from Brad, Louisa, which is why I am placing you together to run a project I've acquired. There's a new microchip we've been testing that provides covert surveillance, almost undetectable to the human eye. It's top secret and there is interest from many organizations, including the government. I need you to develop it and assure its success. Brad will lead and Louisa, you will assist. I've set aside level three for your offices, and the Kryton project staff are at your disposal. That wrapped up last week, so they are ready to go."

He leans back and smiles. "I'm here if you need me, but I want this to be your baby. Prove to me you can do this, and I could be looking at the next CEO of Technofad."

The fact he's looking at Brad as he speaks causes my blood to chill because what the fuck is happening? Who the hell is Brad Turner, anyway, and why do I suspect I've been pushed aside for a stranger?

My father looks at his watch and says quickly, "I'll leave you to get acquainted. I must run to another meeting. Head down to level three and make yourselves at home. We'll meet same time tomorrow for a catch up."

He doesn't even glance at me and merely slaps Brad on the back and leaves me with so many questions I don't know where to begin.

As soon as the door closes, Brad turns to me and says briskly, "Ok, we need to be the best. Failure is not an option, so if you have any nail or hair appointments or brunch dates, cancel them. Office hours are seven am until nine pm and I expect no extended lunch breaks and distractions. We work hard to play hard later. Any questions?"

I stare at him with my mouth open because since when was he the boss of me?

My eyes flash as I say curtly, "Firstly, contrary to what you just said, I don't schedule personal appointments in my working day. I don't even take a lunch period and my only distraction is my desire to succeed. Secondly, I don't appreciate being told how to organize my day with no discussion and thirdly, I may be detailed with assisting you, but I will not be made to feel like the hired help. I've worked hard to gain my father's respect through grit and determination and if you believe I'm some empty-headed heiress with cotton candy between her ears, then we've got a problem–Brad." I spit his name like it personally insults me, and his amused smile rubs me up the wrong way.

"Noted, Louisa. But if you want my respect, you earn it. I'm sure the same goes for me." He leans over the table and fixes me with an intense stare that makes me uncomfortable.

"We will work well together. I heard you were a tough one to crack and consider the challenge accepted."

He actually winks and stares at me as if he wants to rip my clothes off and smirks, "This is going to be so good. I'm going to enjoy having you under me, Louisa, and you are welcome to try to make it on top."

He winks, making me feel as if a thousand bugs are crawling across my skin and then he kicks back his chair and nods to the door. "Level three it is."

As he stands back to let me pass, I'm pretty certain it's just to check out my ass and the anger builds inside me as I anticipate a very difficult few months ahead.

CHAPTER 12

FLYNN

I've imagined having a mother so many times it's become part of my daily routine. Now I have one, it's a little surreal and as we take a walk around her beautiful home, she asks me many questions and appears to hate the answers. I can't pretend I had an apple pie upbringing. Even though I tone it down out of respect for her sanity, it's pretty obvious I had an abused childhood. The devastation in her eyes hurts me deeply and as we sit overlooking the waterway, I say sadly, "It was hard being alone. I never had anyone, only Wesley. I learned to accept my own company and only really understood the value of friendship when I was sent to college."

Somehow, we are now holding hands and it's kind of nice. Sitting on a grassy bank watching nature, beside the person I never believed existed. I must be in paradise. It certainly feels that way.

I can tell my past upsets her, so I turn the conversation to her. "Tell me about Iris Young. Dimitri told me she was his governess."

"Apparently so." Vivian looks confused. "I met her after I

gave birth. She came to the hospital with flowers and told me she was sent by Massimo."

She shivers with revulsion. "I told her to get out. I never wanted to even think of him again, but she ignored me and pulled the curtains before telling me she was going to give me a fresh start. I had nothing, Flynn. I couldn't go back to work at the bar; that was never an option. She told me that now the baby had died, all the support from Wesley would stop. My family had disowned me, and I had no money and no place to live. Iris Young reached into her bag and handed me an envelope. She told me it contained a plane ticket to Seattle, enough to rent a small apartment for three months and a job offer from Technofad industries. I was being paid off, her words not mine, and she told me if I knew what was good for me, I would take this opportunity and never look back."

"You had no choice; I can see that."

"So I thought, however…"

She stares at me through troubled eyes and whispers, "I was a fool, Flynn. I believed everything I was told. I never even got to hold you in my arms. They told me you had died in my womb and had sent you to the mortuary. All I was required to do was sign my name on the death certificate and the discharge papers, and I was free to go. I was so naïve. I never questioned any of it and if I had asked more questions, perhaps things would have been so different."

As she speaks, my mind starts working quickly and I squeeze her hand and say sadly, "You are not to blame. Neither of us are. We were the victims of a professional bully and never stood a chance."

Turning to face her, I try to drag my mind back to the practicalities because I'm not sure how much more emotion I can take. "We should take a DNA test."

Her eyes widen and she shakes her head. "I don't need a…"

"Neither do I but Dimitri may prefer this done properly. We

should arrange it and then I'll return home and grab what I need to test Wesley."

"You're going back."

She looks absolutely horrified about that, and I shrug. "I must. Now that I've found you, I want to make things right. It's important to determine who my father is. Something is telling me it's not the man you think it is."

"Wesley?" She looks as if she's going to hurl, and I sigh heavily. "It's exactly what he would have done. Hell, he does it for fun most nights, anyway."

"Rape!" Vivian is shocked and I nod, the bitterness apparent in my words as I snap, "He's a bastard and has never changed. For whatever reason, he wanted you to believe Massimo was the rapist, and I was dead. He protects himself in every way. Always making out it's someone else, so the blame can never be directed at him. Possibly he wanted a son to torment, to build in his image and I was the unlucky result of that."

"Don't!" Vivian sounds angry, and I stare at her in surprise.

"Don't ever doubt that you are anything but amazing, Flynn. You have become a man who I'm proud to call my son under the harshest of circumstances. That's not easy and you deserve credit for that. You do what you must. Set yourself free and then you come straight back to me because I don't want to waste a minute more of my life without you in it and I will devote the rest of mine to being the mother I always should have been."

The tears are running like rivers down her face, and she wipes them away with a fierceness that makes me smile. Impulsively, I pull her close and hold her in my arms and love how my heart fills with love for the first time in my life. I let her in, and she sets up residence because she's right. Now we have found one another, I pity the poor bastard who tries to tear us apart.

* * *

We make a stop at the medical center and take our DNA tests. It's purely to clarify something we both know already and as we leave with the results of that, it reaffirms that we were right.

We head toward Technofad, where Vivian is meeting Dimitri for lunch, and she has invited me to tag along. She texted Dimitri to ask Louisa to join us, which I am more than happy about. In fact, I am looking forward to it more than I expected, which makes the DNA test on Wesley even more urgent because if he is my father, I'm coming back for Louisa as well as Vivian.

While we wait in reception, I tap out a message to Malik. I should have done this earlier, but it was more important to talk with Vivian. However, now I need answers and so I ask him to find Iris Young, giving him everything I discovered about her. If anyone can find her, Malik can and I'm expecting the information by return. I don't understand how he does it. He's always been able to discover anything and who knows what surveillance he had set up around campus at Rockwell Academy. I suppose it's his area of expertise. Most of us are experts in violence. Malik prefers carefully controlled torture and technology. He would fit in well at Technofad, I'm certain of that.

It's not long before Dimitri shows up with a strangely subdued Louisa in tow, who looks so angry I wonder what happened this morning. Vivian must notice it too because she says with concern, "Are you ok, honey?"

Dimitri offers a slight shake of his head in a warning and Vivian looks worried when Louisa says with a hint of bitterness, "If you don't mind, I'll skip lunch today."

Her parents share a look, and my anger rises at the idea anyone has upset my girl, because she is my girl and it's only a matter of time before everyone else knows that.

My phone vibrates with a text, and I shake my head in disbelief. Fuck that man, he's a legend and I say quickly, "I'm sorry, I'll have to skip lunch too. Something came up."

"Are you sure?" Vivian looks disappointed and I say softly, "I'll meet you back here in an hour, or whenever you're ready. I have a few calls to make."

"But you should eat." I smile because I'm loving experiencing the concern of a mother for her son. Turning to Louisa, I say casually, "Perhaps you could direct me to the nearest coffee shop, and I'll grab a sandwich. You can join me if you like."

She looks up and I want to smash someone at the hurt in her eyes and she nods, "Of course. There's one across the street. I'll show you."

Dimitri nods and turns to his daughter and whispers something in her ear and she shrugs and turns away, leaving him looking a little lost and unsure what to do next. Fixing him with a nod, I assure him I'll take care of her and the gratitude in his eyes makes me feel like a god. It's unusual to be the good guy for once in my life and if anyone deserves to be the recipient of that, it's this family.

As they turn and head off to lunch, I wrap my arm around Louisa and love how it makes me feel. "Come on, baby, tell me all about it."

CHAPTER 13

LOUISA

I can't even look at my father. I am so angry. All morning I have endured Brad Turner ordering me around and making me look like the hired help. He made me sit outside his office like an assistant, while he took the only one with a door. He assigned himself a secretary and told me to check in with her every morning to discover my duties. He called a staff meeting and introduced himself as the boss and me as his assistant. Then he proceeded to lay down the law and create an atmosphere of tension that definitely doesn't need to be there.

When my father stopped by to take me to lunch, Brad was all smiles and even walked us to the elevator, telling me to enjoy lunch and not to worry about work for a while. To take a rest so I am fully refreshed for the afternoon. My father sang his praises all the way to ground level and if I hear the name Brad Turner fall from his lips one more time, I'm liable to punch him.

Now I'm walking with Flynn like a couple toward the coffee shop and immediately everything is better in my world. That alone tells me I'm screwed because, in all probability, this guy is my freaking cousin. When did my life fall into hell and how could I have prevented it from happening?

Flynn orders us both an Americano and a bagel each and steers me toward a booth in the corner and then, to my surprise, slides in bedside me and grabs my hand.

"Ok, baby, what happened today to make you angry?"

For some reason, the concern on his face unravels me and unwelcome tears brim behind my eyes as I sniff, "I thought I was better than I am."

"Explain." He looks confused and I fill him in on everything that happened.

He appears thoughtful as I sip my coffee and I immediately feel better for getting it off my chest and then he says casually, "I'll do some digging on him. Guys like that usually have a history and if I can discover his, it may give you something to work with."

"What do you mean?" I'm not sure and he grins with a wicked twist to his lips that makes me smile.

"I've met men like him, baby. They talk themselves up and play the game to hide their own incompetence. The hardest working people don't shout about it, they get on with it and so your problem may be an opportunity to get what you want."

"Do you really think so?"

Flynn appears to have a habit of lifting my spirits and he reaches out and strokes my face with a gentleness that surprises me. The softening of his eyes and the deep velvet gaze of lust make me speechless because suddenly things are shifting between us, and I like it.

I would stare into his eyes all day if I was allowed and as he leans closer, I almost anticipate my first kiss, but how wrong is that? So wrong on every level ever invented and instead he brushes those lips against my ear and whispers, "I'll always be here for you, baby girl. You can tell me anything."

It's so good to be the object of his attention. It's a little overwhelming and yet the most delicious sensation in the world. He wraps me in comfort and makes everything special. I could tell him anything and he would never judge me, I already know that, and it's so good to be in his arms, shut away from reality for just the briefest moment in time.

He looks at his phone and whispers, "I've discovered where Iris Young is."

"No way. Already." My eyes are wide as I glance at his phone, and I see the name Cedar Heights retirement home. Wisteria Falls.

"Where is that?"

"Not far from where I live, actually. It appears I need to return home, quite urgently."

"You do." My face falls, and he tilts it to his and holds it in a tender grip. "Come with me."

The passion burning in his eyes is compelling and I say slightly breathlessly, "How?"

"This weekend. We'll fly back. I have an apartment my uncle doesn't know about, and I have a guest room you can stay in. I promise you will be perfectly safe."

I nod my head because I want to go so badly and whisper, "My father may not allow it."

"Then convince him. You see, Louisa…" He brushes his lips against my ear and whispers, "I need to prove that we're not related, and I'm hoping she holds the answer to that."

"You do." I hold my breath because I don't want to break this spellbound moment and he says huskily, "I'm guessing you understand why."

"Not really." Once again, the tears build and I say sadly, "You see, Flynn, nobody ever wants me, the girl, not the heiress. You say you've been alone all your life, well I kind of understand a lot about that. It's why I have no friends and spend my spare time reading. People want me for what I can give them, not for me. I stand to inherit billions and that's a pretty tempting carrot to any guy. I made up my mind a long time ago that I would settle for nothing less than love, but nobody ever cared enough to try."

"You think I want your billions?"

He looks angry, disappointed even and I shrug, "Why wouldn't I? I mean, you are so out of my league, it's pretty obvious. I'm sorry, Flynn, I'm distrustful for a reason and I am the only person who can protect my heart because nobody else cares."

To my surprise, he holds my face firmly and says angrily, "You know nothing about what I want. What my type is, what attracts me and what I'm looking for. You have judged me like everyone who judges you and labeled me a certain way by looking at me. You don't know me, not really. But I know you, Louisa. I *feel* you."

He holds my hand to his thumping heart and says roughly, "You are everything I want. You are perfect for me. You could be a stripper for all I care because it's what's inside I crave. The beautiful soul of an Angel who doesn't realize how amazing she is. A goddess and a kind soul who isn't tainted by life's shit and rises above it with a pure spirit. It is I who doesn't deserve a woman like you, Louisa. You are way too good for me and if anyone ever makes you believe you don't measure up, then that's their loss, baby, and you should pity their ignorance."

I almost think he's going to kiss me, hard and possessive, in full view of my father's employees. The sad thing is I want him to. Just once. To make me feel invincible because his little speech almost makes me believe it myself.

He is staring at me with such a deep yearning I can't cope with the feelings that creates and so I say breathlessly, "I'll come."

The relief in his eyes lifts my heart and as he rubs his thumb across my lips, he whispers, "I need you with me and I promise until we know for sure, I will treat you like family. If we discover otherwise, well, we'll talk again."

I nod and say with a sigh. "I should head back. Brad doesn't agree with lunch."

"What time do you finish?"

"Nine." I groan as he raises his eyes. "Like fuck you do. I'll come for you at six and if he has a problem with that, he can talk to me about it."

The fierce rage in his eyes makes me smile and I almost pity Brad. It's obvious Flynn sets his own agenda, and it will be interesting to see who wins this one. I kind of already know and so, feeling a lot better about things, I head back to work with a distinct spring in my step.

CHAPTER 14

FLYNN

I use my time wisely. When Louisa heads off back to work, I put in another call to Malik who answers sounding weary.

"How's it going in Seattle?"

"Surprising."

"I don't like surprises."

"Then you're going to hate this one."

"Why?"

His voice shifts and the razors cutting through the phone tell me Malik is struggling like the rest of us. He is currently playing the good son to a father who enjoys torture as a hobby. He is the head of security to the ruler of Dubai and the sinister shit he deals with makes Massimo Delauren look like Santa Claus.

"We may have a problem regarding my marriage."

"Don't tell me. She hated you on sight."

Malik's low laughter makes me smile and I say cockily, "Dream on my friend, we all know I have the golden touch and she is no exception."

"Her father then. He hated you on sight."

"Again, you are wrong, which amuses me because of how much you hate being wrong."

Malik growls with impatience. *"Well, someone must have hated you on sight. Come on, make my day because this one is shaping up to be one from hell."*

"Nobody hates me, except you right now."

My low laugh makes him groan, and he says wearily, *"Then what's the problem?"*

"We could be related."

"How?"

"It turns out my evil uncle told my amazing mother that Massimo Delauren is my father."

Even saying the words strangles my rational mind and Malik's curse tells me he is as shocked as I am.

"And you believe him? I mean, your uncle is hardly the truth fairy."

"My thoughts exactly, which is why Iris Young may have the answers."

"About that."

The hairs on the back of my neck stand up and Malik says with a hint of urgency in his voice, *"I pulled her medical records. She's at early-stage dementia and her medication is strong. You might not get much sense out of her, and it may not be the truth, anyway."*

"Fuck."

I ball my fist and growl, "What else can you tell me?"

"She only has one visitor. Every Friday at two o'clock, Massimo Delauren visits for exactly one hour. He never changes his routine, and they take tea in her room."

"How civilized. Anything else?"

"He donates several hundreds of thousands of dollars to the home every year and is their biggest contributor. The staff love him because he is very generous. Subsequently, Iris Young is treated like a queen because she is their proverbial golden goose and Massimo has requested that she receive no other visitors."

"How do you discover this shit?"

I'm still amazed by that, and Malik's smug laugh makes me smile.

"It's called cybercrime, my friend, and once I hacked into their system, I found everything I needed. There is a list of demands against her file that is password protected and saved in a different folder to the normal residents. Mrs. Travers is the woman who runs it and after a little digging, I have located her Achilles heel."

"And…"

"She has an offshore account with a bottom line that tells me she is way above the pay grade of the usual care home manager. Transfers are made from various sources, and they match deceased residents accounts. It appears that she is being well paid, and the money shows up in the account the day before the residents pass."

"Which means?"

"I'm taking an educated guess that she helps them on their way for a fee."

"I see."

I think hard and Malik says roughly, *"What's your plan?"*

"To find out what Iris Young knows and run a DNA test on Wesley. If I can prove he is my father, as I suspect, then I can carry on with the original plan. If it turns out he was telling the truth for once, I'll probably jump off a cliff rather than share blood with Massimo Delauren."

"We are crafted from monsters and live in their shadow, my friend. It's up to us to be the bigger monster and change the course of history. All that means is you have a more important job than most."

I hate the sympathy in his voice and the reassurances he is trying to give me. If I believed for one moment, I shared a drop of blood with the most deranged man on the planet, I may as well be dead because who knows how that madness will manifest itself in me and I say as a distraction, "I need another favor."

"You always do." Malik sounds weary, but he loves this shit.

"I need information on a guy named Brad Turner who worked at Technofad Washington and has relocated to Seattle."
"What's he to you?"
"Trouble."
"Consider it done."

As he cuts the call, I cast my mind to the care home and the woman who runs it. It appears I will have my work cut out getting past her system and the last thing I want is to alert Massimo to our visit.

I need to think this one through and as I order another coffee, I begin to formulate a plan in my mind.

I MANAGE to pick up a few personal items and then grab a cab back to the house to catch up with Vivian. We spend a pleasant afternoon in her kitchen chatting about shit. She tells me about her family, her life, and her marriage. Despite her beginnings, she is settled now which gives me hope for my own future. Dimitri sounds like a decent guy and I'm happy for her.

Part of me craves a life like this. No problems, just happiness. Maybe not on this scale, but a loving wife and a cozy home where I would feel safe. Then I am transported back to the world I live in and the only way I know how to exist. Even if I do achieve the impossible and set myself free, my job title remains. I am the heir to the Vasquez crime family and am expected to step up as the man in charge when required. Sure, I could turn my back on it, but it's all I know. Along with my brothers, we would enjoy a different kind of business. On our terms. Protecting one another's backs and making sure nobody ever messed with us. World domination, at least that's the plan and the only thing that would make that even more perfect, is if Louisa was by my side.

My thoughts turn to her regularly throughout the afternoon and I pay more attention whenever her name is mentioned. Vivian speaks of her with a smile, and I can tell she loves her like a daughter. I discover everything I can about both sisters and hate the picture that unfolds of one child living a charmed life and the other doing everything she can to avoid it. Like me, Louisa doesn't fit in, and I hate knowing how much that must hurt her.

As the afternoon nears to its close, I say casually, "I have some things to pick up in town. Perhaps I should drop by the office and head back with Louisa."

Vivian nods, seemingly not at all surprised by that.

"You should take my car. It's insured for any driver and Dimitri won't mind. Here."

She tosses me the keys to her Porsche and as I catch them, I say thankfully, "Are you sure?"

"Of course, why wouldn't I? You need to be independent, Flynn, and I want you to feel at home here."

Her words are accompanied by a warm smile, and it hits me hard in the heart. It's her acceptance of me that means the most. The love in her eyes as she adopts her role as my mother and holds nothing back. I never thought it would be this way and for a man who has never experienced anything like this, it's a powerful weapon. If nothing else good comes out of this, it doesn't matter because I have found my mother and in my dreams she was a shadow of the reality because I couldn't have wished for a better one.

CHAPTER 15

LOUISA

I don't know how I'm going to get through this project. I hate Brad Turner and it appears he loves nothing more than putting me in my place and making sure I understand he is the boss.

When I returned from lunch, he looked at his watch and shook his head as if I had disappointed him and just thrust a folder at me and told me to read it and file my report by the close of business.

He then asked Miranda, his assistant, to bring him coffee, and he didn't want to be disturbed, and stormed back into his office and slammed the door.

I thought I had got off lightly until I read through the papers and realized there were weeks of work involved. I didn't even understand what most of it meant and yet the last person I want to admit that to is my new self-styled boss.

So, with a grim determination, I work through it as best I can and am surprised when I hear a husky voice say from the doorway, "Six o'clock, baby, your carriage awaits."

I look up to find the office empty, as it appears the rest of the staff left already. Brad's door is still firmly closed, and

Flynn is regarding me with amusement as he leans against the wall nonchalantly.

My heart quickens when I see how hot he is. His lazy eyes drag the length of me, and his usual black suit makes my mouth water at the sight of him. He has the image of the most successful businessman and is definitely the sexiest, and I still can't wrap my head around the feelings I've developed toward him.

Before I can react, Brad's door flies open and he storms out and then stops suddenly when he sees Flynn, who is regarding him through turbulent eyes. In fact, the tension notches up in an instant and if I were Brad, I would head right back the way I came.

Instead, he says irritably, "Who's this, Louisa?"

It's so embarrassing as he turns his back on Flynn and I open my mouth to answer him, but the reply comes from Flynn before I can.

"I'm the man with a problem, Brad."

Brad spins on his heels and looks at him in surprise, almost as if he didn't believe he could talk.

"A problem. What the fuck are you talking about?"

He turns on me angrily. "Who is this clown, Louisa, because if you're bringing your personal life to work already, we have a problem?"

"Brad, I…" But that's as far as I get because Flynn shifts off the wall and reaches Brad in an instant and before he can react, grabs him by the throat and holds him up in the air in a show of strength that makes my mouth drop.

His voice sounds low and dangerous as he growls, "Now shut the fuck up and listen, because I will only say this once."

He leans in and sneers, "You will treat Louisa with the respect she deserves and stop making her life a misery. She starts work at eight thirty and finishes at six. She has one hour for lunch and two fifteen-minute coffee breaks and that also applies to the rest of the staff. If there is a problem with that, take it up with Dimitri because they are his rules. Secondly, you can the attitude because I'm sure we both agree you have no right to it."

He drops Brad, who clutches his neck and stutters, "What are you talking about?"

Flynn growls, "If you want me to tell Dimitri about your gambling habit, I'm happy to."

Brad stares at me and I already see the defeat in his eyes, but he says quickly, "I don't know what you are talking about."

Flynn shakes his head as if disappointed somehow. "I thought you might say that. Well, it's come to my attention that you were a regular at the Domino bar in Washington. Have I jogged your memory yet?"

I watch in fascination as Brad turns a strange color and Flynn laughs darkly.

"It appears you owe them rather a lot of money and the interest alone is staggering. I happen to be acquainted with the guy who runs it and he's not a patient man and I'm guessing would be very interested to add your new address to his contacts."

Brad turns white as Flynn growls, "Maybe he already knows, and you struck a deal."

"No." Brad's voice comes out in a rough whisper, and I stare at him in confusion. Flynn shakes his head slowly and looks at him with disgust.

"You see, I had an interesting conversation with him earlier today and it appears you promised him you would soon have access to billions."

He flicks a soft look in my direction, and I can sense what's coming as he says angrily, "Yes, he told me you had your sights set on a promotion and failing that had two shots at marrying an heiress. Apparently, one would be grateful, and the other is so stupid she would thank you for it."

I feel nauseous as Flynn tells me something I've lived with ever since puberty. It's always the same story. Men want Sienna because she's easier on the eye and would be happy to fall into her role as a society wife. I'm the second prize and the one who should be grateful that I'm asked. It's why I'm so guarded and allow nobody close and yet hearing it happening again doesn't make me feel good about myself.

Brad says angrily, "You're wrong. You're making this up to suit yourself."

Flynn takes out his phone and hisses, "Shall we call Jonny and ask him, because I'm guessing he will back up my story?"

"What do you want?" Brad already sounds defeated and Flynn shrugs. "I couldn't give a fuck how much trouble you're in, but there is one thing that is never going to happen. You are not marrying into this family, and you will work your ass off to pay back the money through hard work because if you step out of line, Dimitri gets all the facts, and you probably won't have a job. Then I'll find you and deliver you to Jonny personally and, as a favor to me, he will show you the error of your ways. So…"

He turns to me and says lightly, "Get your purse, baby, your day is done."

As I rush to my feet, Flynn says casually, "Oh and another thing…"

He takes my hand and pulls me beside him and says ominously, "You treat Louisa with respect and if I see one shadow in her eyes when she returns home from work, I'll hold you responsible and our next meeting won't be so pleasant. Understand?"

Brad nods in defeat. "Of course. I'm sorry, Louisa."

"It's…" I don't know what to say and Flynn laughs out loud. "Well, hasn't this been fun? Have a good evening, Brad, and word of advice, stay away from the clubs, stick to what you're good at, which is making money, not losing it."

As I follow Flynn from the office, I'm in awe of him. Seeing him tear Brad roughly from his pedestal gave me a rush I wasn't expecting. I loved it. The cruel way he humiliated him and exposed him in a few sentences. The defeat in Brad's eyes and the sick expression on his face made me happy. Now I understand why every girl loves a bad boy, because that show of domination has caused every one of my lady parts to throb with heated desire. If the guy wasn't my freaking cousin, I would have jumped him by now, which tells me I have a serious problem and its name is Flynn Vasquez.

CHAPTER 16

FLYNN

I'm not sure how we managed it, but three days later we are on a private jet heading back to Los Angeles. Louisa managed to convince her father that she should accompany me home because she had some meetings set up regarding their new project. He agreed and offered up the company jet and so here we are bound for home and hopefully the answer that we both desire more than anything.

Over the past three days, we have grown closer, and I have loved spending time with my new family. Louisa has been happier at work now Brad has been warned off and I spent glorious time with my mother while dodging Sienna's endless invitations to show me off to her friends.

"This is nice." Louisa stretches out opposite me and smiles sweetly, and I swear my heart skips a beat. I can't help desiring her. She is everything I love. Funny, smart and completely unaware of her natural beauty that manifests itself every time she looks my way.

We have a connection that we can't ignore, which is why this weekend is going to be an extreme test of resistance.

"It's been so long since I went to LA."

"I didn't know you had."

I take a swig of the whiskey offered to me in a crystal glass by the company stewardess.

"Yes, my father had a house there, possibly because that's where he originated from. Not that they visited much. I'm guessing the bad memories kept them away. We spent the odd vacation there until he sold it and bought a penthouse instead. I've never been there. As I said, it's been a long time."

I'm grateful he does because now we won't have to head to my own apartment, which I'm a little relieved about. Not that I'm ashamed of my modern sterile penthouse, but it's always been my escape from life. Nobody ever goes there, which is what I like. I wasn't sure how I'd cope with another person in my personal space and it's best to stay in unfamiliar territory for both of us.

I laugh softly. "I still can't believe you persuaded your father."

She giggles, which makes me smile. "Probably because he's feeling guilty about Brad. He could tell I was upset, and he would never admit it, but he would agree to anything to make me happy."

"I can understand that." I stare at her with a deep yearning that I'm hoping I'm hiding well because this is pure torture. More than anything, I want to experience what Louisa tastes like. She is like the most tempting forbidden fruit hanging just out of reach.

My motto has always been one night only for a very good reason. Emotion. I don't react well to that and yet I've always had a deep yearning for a connection with someone, probably because it's always been denied to me.

Now I have everything I want except for one thing. Louisa could be my cousin and related by blood. Which is why I'm so eager to discover the truth because I stand to gain much more than the relief at not sharing DNA with a psychopath.

By the time we touch down, I'm desperate for answers. This weekend is going to be torturous enough sharing an apartment with Louisa. I'm not sure how I'll stop myself from touching her, desperate for one lick, one swipe of the tongue to satisfy this carnal urge that is consuming me.

I know it's not me either. It's her. She wants me too and I can tell that by the unguarded lust in her eyes when she thinks I'm not looking. The blush to her cheeks as she looks away and the rapid breathing when I brush against her or take her hand. We are dancing a complicated tango and I just hope we get to finish it because how will I recover from this aching need if it turns out I can't have her?

* * *

DIMITRI HAS ARRANGED a car and a driver, and we are soon heading into town, and I'm not surprised when we pull up outside the most luxurious hotel in LA and discover Dimitri's penthouse within its luxurious walls.

Louisa looks tired and, as the doorman helps the driver with our bags, I take her hand and walk proudly beside her inside.

Once we retrieve the key, we take the elevator to the final floor and, as it opens, we step into the purest luxury.

"This is amazing."

Louisa's eyes are wide as she stares around at paradise, and I must agree. Obviously, Dimitri appointed the finest designers and as we stare at the modern trappings of success, I'm even more determined to live this life myself.

The finest art and the most exquisite furniture adorn a huge loft style apartment that's boasts the city as a backdrop, courtesy of the floor to ceiling windows that reveal the city outside.

"I wonder why I haven't been here before now?" Louisa says

with disappointment. "In fact. This is one of several my father owns but rarely steps foot inside."

"It's impressive. I can't argue with that."

Louisa sighs and looks troubled.

"What?" I'm quick to ask and she says slightly bitterly, "It's just a waste. All of this money tied up in a museum piece that rarely sees life. How is this right when so many have so little?"

"Says the daughter of a billionaire."

She turns and I love how her eyes flash with a temper that stirs my interest even further.

"What's that supposed to mean?"

"It means you know shit."

I'm being deliberately cruel, but I can't help it and say roughly, "The world is full of injustice, baby, and you are one of the lucky ones. You enjoy a privileged life and yet feel bad about that. You tell me other people deserve more. Well, of course they do. Nobody deserves to live with no food, no money, and no home to call their own. Nobody deserves to beg for food and worry about where their next meal will come from. There is pain and suffering in the world and there is absolutely nothing you can do about that, except cleanse your own conscience by holding charity fundraisers and doing your bit. Admirable but not enough and you know what, it will never be enough and there will always be somebody richer, somebody with more and people who waste their money and that will never change. So, darlin', step off your soap box and be grateful for what you do have and live your best life, but never judge how other people choose to spend their money until you have your own to make your own choices."

"You think I'm a hypocrite."

She faces me down and I'm loving the passion blazing from her eyes.

"Aren't you? I mean, we flew here in a private jet, for fuck's sake. You agreed to stay in your father's penthouse, and you have a credit account that knows no limits. When was the last time you did something good for someone who needed it?"

"I…" She looks for an answer and the defeat in her eyes tells me I hit the mark.

"Exactly. You have noble thoughts but do fuck all about it. Don't beat yourself up about it, baby. We all live the life fate dealt us and just be grateful yours is better than most."

She looks down and I say gently, "If it's any consolation, I'm worse than you."

Stepping toward her, I lift her pretty face to mine and whisper, "I have money. More money than I can spend, and I get it from crime. I ruin lives for a living, and I benefit financially from that. I give nothing back and I take. I am a monster because I don't give a fuck because this is the law of the jungle and if I don't do it, somebody else will. Things won't change if I turn to religion and dedicate my life to helping others. There will always be a man like me in a dark suit calling the shots. There will always be a man profiteering from other people's misery and there will always be someone more powerful than me. So, I embrace what I am, and I deal with it. I take the money and I couldn't give a fuck. Does that make me a bad man? Of course it does, but in my heart, I am just trying to survive. I am a victim of my birth as much as you are, and that doesn't stop me wanting a better life."

She shifts a little closer. "What is that better life for you, Flynn? What would make you happy?"

I can't help myself and reaching out, I let her soft hair filter through my fingers and her erratic breathing makes me lose my mind.

"I want to be able to love you, Louisa. Not as family, but as something more. To see what it's like to give and receive love. To wake up beside someone who completes you. Not to be afraid of the shadows and to laugh. Feel a happiness that I believe love can give you. To watch my seed grow and create another person and devote my life to making theirs happy. To laugh, to love and to grow old because in my line of work, growing old is a long shot."

To my surprise, she reaches out and touches my face, flattening her palm against my cheek, facing me with eyes awash with tears.

"I like the sound of your dream, Flynn. Do you think dreams can come true sometimes?"

I place my own hand over hers and whisper, "I think they can."

We are so close one move would be all it takes to brush my lips against hers and descend into hell and so with superhuman strength, I pull back and say thickly, "It's late. We should get some sleep because tomorrow will be difficult."

As I break away, she nods and then says sadly, "There are two guest rooms. If you need any food, dad told me to order room service. He has an account with the hotel, and he will settle up."

I nod and as we part ways and make our reluctant way to our respective rooms, tomorrow can't come soon enough for me.

CHAPTER 17

LOUISA

This is pure torture. Alone in an apartment with Flynn, and he's strictly out of bounds. It could have been so different if he knew who his father was. Part of me doesn't care about that, and yet the decent part cringes at the thought of sharing my body with a family member. That will never be an option and it's ironic that I've waited so long to find someone and when it finally happens, there's the largest barrier in the way.

Somehow, I manage to fall asleep, but my dreams are plagued by restless ones and in them all Flynn is running away from me.

GROANING, I slam my hand down on the alarm and blink against the morning light.

It takes a minute to remember where I am and as it all comes back to me, my heart flutters when I remember what happened here last night. I can tell Flynn wants me, and it's reciprocated. Maybe today we will finally learn the truth and I'm impatient for that.

I quickly shower and dress in a smart dress and heels because our first stop is to Cedar Heights retirement home to visit Iris Young. Flynn told me she won't be expecting visitors because Massimo always visits on Friday and today is Saturday. We have a plan to gain access and my heart is thumping with excitement at spending the entire day acting as a couple with Flynn.

The plan is we are married and looking for a home for his ailing aunt. We heard of Cedar Heights and were impressed by the good reports. We also discovered the manager is away on vacation and Flynn is confident we can gain access to Iris Young without anyone suspecting a thing.

As soon as I head into the living room, my heart flutters when I see the man himself sitting at a table by the huge panoramic window. My mouth dries when I see him at his most casual. Black jeans and a smart black button-down polo shirt. The ink on his arms is like a magnet to me and it's difficult to tear my mind from the gutter it's living in right now and his lust-filled eyes that beckon me toward him like a moth to the light, makes me wet because this man is an alpha male of the darkest kind.

"I ordered breakfast. I hope I got it right."

I look with interest at the array of dishes on the table and my mouth waters as I smell the soft pancakes loaded with syrup.

"It beats the fruit I usually have."

I smile and take the seat opposite him, and groan as I stare at the decadent buffet before my eyes. "I wish I had an actual metabolism. You're a sadist, Flynn."

The fact he's eating one of the desirable pancakes makes me stare with longing and he shrugs. "Eat what you like. Life's too short."

"Easy for you to say."

I reach for a fruit cocktail and sigh. "It's ok for people like you and Sienna. I just have to look at these pancakes and I gain several pounds. I even had a personal trainer for a while, and do you know how much I lost?"

"No?"

"Three pounds."

I pull a face and he laughs as I sigh heavily.

"All that effort for little gain. It would be easier to have an operation."

"You are perfect as you are."

"Thank you, but you're only being kind."

Flynn shrugs. "There's just more of you to love. I kind of like you just the way you are."

The fork hovers against my lips as I digest his sweet words. "So, you love me then." I wink to cut the tension that's building, and Flynn laughs out loud.

"Of course, I love you, Louisa. I just don't know in what capacity yet."

"Oh." His words stop me in my tracks, and he leans forward and stares deeply into my eyes.

"Hopefully, we discover that soon."

"Hopefully." I smile into his eyes and see the desire winking back at me. Yes, this could be a very challenging visit and yet for the first time I am loving life and am more alive than I've ever been before.

* * *

CEDAR HEIGHTS RETIREMENT home is more like a palace. In fact, I feel like a princess already because as soon as we left my father's penthouse, Flynn hailed a cab, and we headed across town to his own apartment. We never had time to go inside, but we picked up probably the coolest car I have ever had the pleasure of riding in, and it suits him perfectly. An impressive black Ferrari with cream leather seats looks personally styled to suit his own dark image. Cool, sleek, with a hint of menace, hiding an opulent, stylish interior that wraps you in comfort.

The joy he gets from opening up the engine on the quieter roads makes me smile as we leave the town behind and head for the open countryside.

Just for a moment, I experience freedom like any other girl my age. It's so good to sit beside a man like Flynn and, more than anything, I hope we get the answers we need today.

It's not long before we sweep through large, pillared gates and a sprawling mansion reveals itself through the trees.

"Wow, this place is impressive. Massimo must have really loved Iris Young." I can't help gawping in awe as we register the most amazing place in acres of parkland.

Flynn appears deep in thought. "It will be interesting to see if she shares the same sentiment."

"Do you think she will tell him we were here?"

I'm a little worried about that because, from the few details I learned about my uncle, none of it is good.

Flynn shrugs. "I couldn't give a fuck if she does. That man is fast approaching his use by date."

His words cause a prickle of fear to race through my body, and his low growl sounds ominous.

"It won't be long before we have everything we need to bring the bastard down, and the only thing I want to discover right now is that he's not my father."

"Same." I smile with an encouragement I certainly don't feel inside and as we pull into one of the visitor's bays, my own heart starts racing with a terrible sense of disaster just around the corner.

Flynn asks me to wait, and I'm surprised when he opens my door and offers his hand with a smile. "Allow me, my lady."

It makes me laugh at the chivalrous gesture because he

looks far from that. Despite toning down the menace a little, he still exudes danger, and a tingle of desire passes through me that never seems to go away.

As his hand closes around mine, I sigh inside, wishing this was real.

We walk the short distance to the main entrance and despite the nerves and feeling as if we're doing something wrong, I am more alive than I've ever been and as we ring the doorbell and hear footsteps approaching, I wonder what state I'll be in when the door closes behind us in approximately one hour's time.

CHAPTER 18

FLYNN

A strange sense of calm has descended over me, and it's as if this is happening to someone else. Meeting my mother was possibly the best experience of my life, but meeting Iris Young could prove to be one of the worst.

I'm still unsure how to play this because I'm not aware of how far into dementia she has fallen, but as we stand waiting, I am grateful that for once I'm not doing it alone.

Louisa's hand in mine is comforting, thrilling and as if it was made to fit. It's as if she was always meant to be standing beside me and that is what I'm most nervous about. What if I can't have her?

That one sentence has become the most important one in my life because the more time I spend in her company, the deeper the ache grows. I want her so badly I'm thinking of nothing else and that alone has surprised me.

I've always craved a gentle soul, and she appears the gentlest I've met. Unlike the others, though, I want her for more than one night only and that's what's tearing me apart. What if I'm denied even one night? I'm not sure why it's become so important to me for that at least. Possibly because of the emotions I'm experiencing with my newfound knowledge. Or is it just her? The one I've been searching for only to lose as soon as she is found.

Steeling myself for more disappointment, I nod to the woman who answers the door and regards us with suspicion.

"Um, can I help you?"

She looks nervous and I'm guessing that's because of me, so I let Louisa do the talking as we agreed.

"Mr. and Mrs. Santiago." Louisa beams, holding my hand tightly. "I think you are expecting us."

"Of course." The woman visibly relaxes under Louisa's warm smile and steps aside to let us pass.

"Follow me. I understand you are here about a relative who may wish to make Cedar Heights her home."

"Yes. We've been searching for the best possible place for her and have almost given up hope."

The woman smiles, looking a lot more relaxed.

"Even though I'm biased, you won't find a better place for your relative to live out her days."

I drop back as Louisa charms the woman and cast my eyes over a palatial care home that only the wealthiest residents could ever afford. It's clean, bright and has no trace of the smell these places usually have seeping from their walls. Not that I've been in many but had the misfortune to visit a few when the elderly relative of someone on our radar proves to be an invaluable tool of persuading their relative to give us what we want.

Louisa chats easily to the woman and after we fill in our contact form, making sure to use false information, I hear Louisa says in her gentle voice. "I would love to chat to one of the female residents about their time here. Would that be possible?"

"I don't see why not."

I quickly interrupt. "What was the name of the woman your aunt told you about? Wasn't she her governess at some point?"

"You're right." Louisa turns to the woman and says casually, "I think her name was Mrs. Young. Iris Young to be correct. Do you have a resident by that name living here?"

She looks surprised. "Yes, we do, but she's an extremely private person."

"Oh, that's a shame because it would be so lovely to pass on the kind messages my aunt gave us."

Louisa turns to me and says ruefully, "It would be so lovely for Aunt Ellen to meet a friend here. It would make all the difference."

The woman obviously senses a deal breaker heading her way and I'm guessing wants nothing more than presenting her boss with another resident to inflate their bank balance and I watch with amusement as she seizes her chance and says quickly, "I'm sure it will be fine. If you follow me, Iris has one of our best rooms at the top of the building overlooking the fountain."

We head upstairs and I hold my breath the entire time.

Louisa is acting so cool, and I am extremely impressed with how she conducts herself. I'm certain that's why the woman is agreeing to this, and I'm also guessing her manager wouldn't be quite so accommodating.

As we follow her down a carpeted hallway smelling of freshly cut flowers, I wonder what we will find.

We stop outside the last door in the corridor, and she smiles. "I'll just check she's ok with visitors. If you don't mind waiting here for a second."

"Of course not, we appreciate your help." Louisa smiles at her warmly as she opens the door with a cheery, "It's only me, Iris. Are you up for a couple of visitors?"

As the door slams behind her, I glance at Louisa and wink

and she grins, the flush to her face telling me she's loving every second of this.

We don't speak in case we are overheard, and it's not long before the door opens, and the woman pops her head out. "It's fine. She seemed quite excited about it, poor love. She only usually has one visitor, so it will make a nice change." She laughs gaily. "She even made me apply her lipstick and brush her hair before I came and got you."

Laughing, she holds the door open wide and then stares at her phone as it vibrates in her hand. "Sorry, duty calls. Will you be ok here for about ten minutes or so? I would stay, but this is an emergency."

"It's fine." Louisa smiles warmly. "We won't tire her out."

"Thanks, we're so short staffed it's becoming impossible to…" She stops, looking mortified that her reckless words may have cost her a new resident and I say casually, "We understand and if anything, are more impressed that you provide such a welcoming home for your guests."

She blushes a little and almost backs away from me, causing Louisa to raise her eyes and twist her lips to hide the grin.

As the woman walks quickly away, we waste no time and head inside a pleasant room, overlooking the garden with a fountain, resplendent in a sparkling lake outside.

However, the frail looking woman sitting upright in the chair by the window commands our attention because even as she nears the end of her days, Iris Young has an energy that demands respect.

"Come in and stop dawdling, children."

Her curt voice makes us head inside quickly, and she says sharply, "Stand before me so I can look at you."

Louisa is trying hard not to laugh as we stand like naughty kids before the principal, and she peers over her glasses and shakes her head.

"Stand up straight, girl, and stop slouching. Good posture is the best lesson you will ever learn." Her eyes swivel to me and she frowns and clicks her lips. "Goodness me, those rings must go and what on earth possessed you to scratch ink on your skin. Wear a long-sleeved shirt next time you visit with a tie; yes, a tie is always necessary when visiting."

She points to a chair beside hers and says coolly to me, "You will have to stand." I nod and watch as Louisa takes the spare seat and Iris Young regards us sharply.

"What do you want to know?"

For a moment I'm a little taken aback and Louisa says quickly, "We understand you are acquainted with a friend of ours."

"Possibly. What's their name?"

I'm beginning to wonder if Iris does suffer from dementia because she appears as sharp as my hunting knife and I hold my breath as Louisa says, "Massimo Delauren."

I watch keenly for Iris's reaction and am surprised to see a softening in her expression as she smiles, which relaxes her hard features almost immediately.

"My lovely boy. Yes, he is my son."

Now I hear the dementia shouting at me loud and clear because I have researched their family and know that Massimo and Dimitri's parents were two different people entirely.

Louisa looks confused and Iris leans back and beams with pride. "Yes, he's such a good boy. He comes to see me once a week and I love hearing his beautiful voice. He always was a fine singer and loves it when I comb his hair as he sings me a lullaby, just like I used to do to him."

What the freaking fuck. The image in my mind right now is making me nauseous and Louisa says kindly, "How lovely. You must be very proud."

"Oh, I am my dear, he is such a good man."

I almost laugh out loud and then she whispers, "Only to me, though. He isn't so nice to anyone else."

"Not even his son." Louisa throws in a curve ball, and I feel as if my heart is about to give out on me.

Iris looks confused. "A son?"

Louisa nods. "I understand he had a son who must be in his early twenties now. At least that was what my aunt told me."

"Your aunt?" Iris looks at her sharply and Louisa says without skipping a beat, "Yes, Vivian Clark."

I watch the blood drain from Iris's face as she hears a name she wasn't expecting, and to my surprise, the tears well up in her eyes as her voice breaks. "You know Vivian?"

Louisa nods and smiles kindly. "Yes, she has a son, too."

Iris looks up in shock. "I know."

My mind is on red alert as I wait for the answer I need, and Louisa says in a breathless whisper, "Massimo's son."

Iris looks surprised and the confusion registers in her eyes.

"Massimo doesn't have a son."

I'm not sure what I was expecting, but the relief is enormous, and I almost need to sit down. Then her next words shock me all over again. "You are mistaken, my dear. Vivian Clark had a son, that is true, but Massimo has a daughter."

CHAPTER 19

LOUISA

I swear I stop breathing and I can't even look at Flynn.

"A daughter." I say it softly and watch Iris's eyes fill with tears.

"Such a tragedy. I don't think I will ever forget that terrible time."

"Why, what happened?"

I'm doing all the talking because Flynn looks as if he can't even speak right now and the emotion is so tangible, I'm surprised Iris doesn't see it for herself.

"Massimo fell in love with Imogen. The most beautiful woman I have ever seen. So lovely, like an angel, and he was besotted with her. I've never seen love like it and, well, it was a happy time."

The fond memories that shine from her eyes make me smile because it's obvious that at one point in his life, Massimo was happy and in love.

Iris's expression grows troubled. "They were to become parents; such a joyous time. Massimo was the happiest I had ever seen him, and it made life easier for everyone. Then Imogen went into labor early and Massimo was out of town. There wasn't time to send for a doctor because her waters broke, and I had to act fast. I delivered the baby myself and she was so beautiful, just like her mother."

Iris breaks off and appears so sad it moves me incredibly. "Out of great joy came great sadness." She stares out of the window as if she is seeing pictures from the past and sighs heavily. "Childbirth cost Imogen her life. She hemorrhaged so badly we couldn't save her. The nearest hospital was far away and by the time the doctor came, it was too late."

"I'm so sorry." The grief in Iris's eyes is hard to bear, and she clenches and unclenches her fist as if that's her coping mechanism.

"I called Wesley. He was the only one who could help me."

I catch Flynn's expression and my heart shatters for him. This story is affecting him so deeply I wish she would stop, but she carries on in a slightly wavering voice. "Wesley turned out to be a great help to me. The fact the baby was a girl became a huge problem. He told me that Massimo wouldn't be able to look at the child without seeing her mother, causing him to be afraid of what he may do to punish her for killing the only woman he ever loved."

"Surely he would love her all the more."

I am so incensed I can't help but speak out and Iris laughs, a dull, brittle laugh of someone who has no silver lining on her cloud.

"Wesley was right. Massimo would be overcome with grief and take it out on the child. We had to act fast. I called a childless couple I used to work for who were desperate. They would raise the child as their own and Massimo would never learn of her existence. Wesley told me he heard of an abandoned child we would swap her with. A boy, the son of a worker from his club called Vivian Clark."

I glance at Flynn with concern because this could erupt into madness in a second, but the tense set to his jaw and the dead eyes that stare at Iris with no emotion, chills me even deeper than any emotional outburst. That expression spells huge trouble for Wesley Vasquez.

Iris sighs. "It was the right thing to do. Wesley arranged everything before Massimo returned and it happened just as he said it would. Massimo became mad with grief. I've never seen anything like it, so much that Wesley told him he would take the boy off his hands, so he didn't have to see him. I will never forget the expression in Massimo's eyes when he told Wesley to make the child's life a living hell. He would burn in it for eternity for causing the death of his beloved wife."

Iris breaks off and changes from the frightened woman she was as she relived her past and smiles. "Where are my manners, I haven't offered you any tea. Did I tell you that Massimo likes me to brush his hair? Such beautiful hair. He will be here soon, I'm sure. You must meet him. He's such an angel."

I notice that Flynn has murder in his eyes and say to Iris quickly, "You mentioned Massimo has a daughter. Can you tell us where she lives? Does she visit you too?"

Iris looks a little confused. "Oh no dear, she doesn't live here anymore."

"Where does she live?"

I keep pressing on because the more information we get, the better and Iris smiles happily. "She lives in England, my dear, with another one of my children. Such a lovely family."

The door opens and the care worker heads into the room, looking flustered.

"I'm sorry I was so long. Mr. Benson had a mild heart attack, and I had to dial 911. I'm very sorry, but we must continue the tour another day. I'm so sorry but well, emergency and everything."

For the first time, Flynn speaks up and says huskily, "Of course, thank you for allowing us to visit. We'll be in touch."

He reaches out and takes my hand and, as his cold fingers wrap around mine, I fear the storm about to break on the horizon. I don't think either of us expected what we found, and it's changed everything.

CHAPTER 20

FLYNN

Make his life a living hell.

I can't focus on anything other than that. Wesley has certainly delivered on his promise because every day of my miserable life, I've suffered at his hands.

The hatred burns so deep I almost feel it singe my soul and break it apart before reforming it into something else entirely. I was taken from a mother who would have loved me, even though she had nothing, and made Massimo think he had a son who was responsible for the death of the woman he loved. What a fucking shit show and I have the starring role.

I am silent and it's only when we are several kilometers aways from Cedar Heights that Louise rests her hand on my arm and says gently, "Are you ok, Flynn? I'm worried about you."

I merely nod because I can't trust myself to speak and she says softly, "Please pull over. We need to talk about this."

Swerving sharply to the side of the road, I turn to her with the madness blazing from my eyes and only the fear in her expression stops me from smashing up my car.

Instead, I ball my fist and bang it onto the steering wheel and shout, "I'm going to fucking kill them both."

Louisa's cool hand on my face stops my rant as she twists it to face hers and the large, emotion filled eyes that stare at me with such compassion, douse the flames just a little.

"We got what we came here for. We have the answer you wanted most in the world. That *we* wanted most in the world. You aren't related to Massimo, Flynn. You're nothing like him."

"Then who is my father, Louisa?"

I stare into her eyes with the hatred burning bright in mine.

"I'm guessing I already know the answer to that which doesn't make me feel any better."

"Wesley?"

She looks worried and I groan, leaning back in my seat. "I would stake my entire bank balance on it. That cunning bastard saw a chance to guarantee his future, and he took it and fuck everyone else."

"What do you mean?" She looks confused and I snap.

"Good old Wesley, from the kindness of his heart, took an abandoned baby and pretended it was Massimo's son to save his precious daughter. Fuck that. Wesley saw a golden opportunity and has made Massimo forever in his debt. He raises his son and makes his life a living hell, earning Massimo's undying loyalty for it. All the time Wesley knows the truth but thinks nothing of using his own son to save his own miserable skin. The fact it was Wesley who subjected Vivian to the most violent rape is exactly what he would do. Hell, he does it most nights for fun and then blows their brains out before they can talk."

Louisa looks away and I regret my words. Just seeing the revulsion and horror on her face breaks me all over again because I put it there. It's like a pail of cold water drenching me back from insanity and I reach out and pull her roughly against me and bury my face in her sweet-smelling hair that has the scent of fresh apples.

"I'm sorry, baby, you don't need the details. I shouldn't have said anything."

To my surprise, she holds me with a fierceness that I wasn't expecting and says firmly, "None of this is your fault, Flynn. You apologize for nothing. We will face this together, and I am always going to be on your side."

Just hearing the words rebuilds a small part of my shattered soul and as I pull back, I drown in deep pools of emotion. Louisa is staring at me as if she wants to take all my pain for herself and as her lower lip trembles and the tears spill down her pretty face, it brings me back to the thing I want the most.

As I run my thumb across her cheek, I wipe the crystal water away from her eyes and whisper huskily, "It turns out we're not related after all."

A tentative smile ghosts her lips, and she whispers, "I think it does."

I stare in wonder at the woman in my arms and now the possibilities for us have changed, I am keen to move things on. However, Louisa is inexperienced. She must be afraid and so I whisper huskily, "I think we should return to the apartment and work things out from there."

As I make to pull away, she reaches out and drags me back to her and the slight flush on her face and her erratic breathing are like the greatest aphrodisiac in the world.

"Not before you kiss me, Flynn."

She blushes as she says the words and I smile.

I can't help dragging my finger across her plump lips as I say huskily, "Are you sure, baby? Do you really want to step over the line with me?"

"I do." She bats those thick lashes and looks like a Botticelli cherub. So innocent, so sweet, and so tempting.

Then, as I hold her face in my hands, I lean closer and brush my lips against hers. Just touching them against mine is the most powerful experience and as I deepen the kiss, her lips part willingly and the sweep of my tongue stakes a claim on her that I will never surrender. Louisa is my woman, finally, and I will treasure every moment of this.

Our tongues twist in the most glorious dance of discovery and as we lean closer and my hand wraps around the back of her head, I show her how desirable she is. I feast on her. I consume her and I own every part of that mouth and pulling her lower lip between my teeth, I bite down gently, and her moan of passion is the sweetest sound. As kisses go, this one is the best I've ever had because it's the start of something I have longed for all my life. It's only her family I need to persuade now because it's obvious Louisa wants the same as me and as we kiss after the most tumultuous hour of my life, she brings me right back down and calms my spirit. She has chased away the madness and replaced it with soft, sweet love.

We must kiss for a good thirty minutes before I reluctantly pull back and say softly, "We should return to the apartment. Things have changed and we need to discuss what that means for us."

"Us?"

I hear the concern mixed with longing in her voice and I nod with a resolve that will never break.

"Yes, Louisa. I want you in my life and not as my fucking cousin, either. I want us to be a proper couple and I want to marry you."

"Marry me."

She sounds shocked and I say with determination. "Yes, baby. I'm not fooling around here. I knew from the moment I saw you I wanted to marry you and now the green light is flashing, I see no sense in holding back from that."

"You say you have the green light. What if I have other ideas?"

Her teasing tone tells me she's playing, and I grin. "Then I'll have to persuade you, won't I?"

"You will." Her soft chuckle makes me smile and knowing she's happy drives the last shadow away. There are no shadows when she's around. She's the light in my life that illuminates the dark corners and chases the monsters away. She calms my spirit and makes me a better man and I already know how important she is to me. Now I need to persuade her that she can't live without me and that will be my pleasure because making this woman happy has now become my number one priority.

CHAPTER 21

LOUISA

I don't know if I've ever been happier. In fact, it's heaps better than I thought it would be. We are free to be together. It hit me as soon as Iris Young told us Massimo didn't have a son. The relief was enormous despite the devastating tale she then went on to spill. I can't begin to imagine how Flynn must be coping right now with what we heard. Just the swirl of emotions in his eyes told me it wasn't a happy place to be. But now, the cloud has lifted, and there is hope on the horizon. It turns out we're not related after all, and I am excited to discover what that means for us.

We make our way back to the penthouse and now I'm nervous for a different reason entirely. There are no barriers in our way save for one. My virginity.

I'm so ashamed about that and worried about what Flynn will think. I'm guessing he's used to experienced women who model lingerie for a living. Just imagining him looking at my own large body fills me with anxiety because what the fuck am I playing at? Men like Flynn don't date women like me, not willingly, anyway.

The niggling doubt that just won't go away taunts me all

over again. 'He only wants your inheritance, you stupid bitch.' I wish that voice wasn't talking on repeat most days. It's been there all my life because nothing has ever proven it wrong. From early on, I learned people only wanted to be my friend because of my family connections. I was invited to all the parties in the hope of a decent gift and my father's business contacts.

Other girls would pretend to be my friend because their parents made them and sniggered behind my back because I wasn't as pretty as them. Even my own sister joined in, and I have spent many hours fighting the demons that are always present, knowing that I will never be one of them. Accepted for who I am because I don't look good in fashion. Because I don't speak the same language and the fact no boy would ever want me other than for a step up the ladder. I built an emotional wall to keep the hurt away. It would only affect me if I let it and so I gained a different reputation. I was rude, belligerent, and unfriendly. Sharp, vicious, and cold. I was none of those things, but the moment I stood up for myself and decided I wouldn't play by their rules, I was dropped like a hot stone and left to sit on the table at lunch on my own. The party invites dried up and the looks I got were disapproving ones. I knew what they were saying behind my back. 'She thinks she's above us.' 'Who does she think she is?' 'Louisa Sullivan is an ice princess and no fun.'

No, I have never fitted in, which is why I'm finding it hard to comprehend that Flynn likes me for anything other than what I can give him and not for the first time, it hurts like hell.

"Hey, you've gone quiet on me, baby."

Flynn's husky voice interrupts my painful thoughts as he cuts the engine in the underground car park of the hotel. The dim artificial light glows around us and I shrink into the shadows in the hope of never having to reveal the extent of my pain.

"I was thinking." I force a brightness in my voice that has always served me well over the years.

"What about?"

He sounds curious and I sigh heavily. "About work."

"Work?"

His low laughter makes me smile. "Why is that funny?"

"Because we have just listened to a horror story and the only thing on your mind is work."

If anything, he sounds pained about that and it upsets me. Reaching out, I grab his hand and say slightly hesitantly, "I'm sorry, Flynn. I lied."

"Why?" he seems genuinely confused and I lean back and shake my head sadly. "If you must know, I was thinking about you."

"And that put a frown on your face. I don't like hearing that."

"No, it wasn't anything you've done, the opposite, in fact. I suppose it's my own insecurities coming out and slapping me around the face again. Telling me this is too good to be true and you are only interested in me for what I can give you."

"Is that what you think?" He sounds angry and I shrug.

"When you've lived as me, you kind of expect it. I've never known any different. You see, all my life, people have tolerated me because of who my father is. They never wanted to get to know me. They just wanted the connection and it's hard to think otherwise when you've lived with that reality all your life."

To my surprise, a soft hand tilts my face to a very concerned looking one, and he says fiercely, "I'm not most people, Louisa. I make my own rules and fuck what people say. You know, all my life I've had no one. Like you, its defined who I am, and I built my defenses well. People only wanted me for the danger, the excitement, and the reputation. I deal with shit most of the time and seek an angel to restore my faith in humankind."

"An angel?"

I'm confused, and he rubs his thumb across my lips and says huskily. "I'm only interested in what's inside. I love a kind, gentle soul much more than a pretty doll. I determine beauty in the goodness of someone's heart. The way they treat others and the kindness they show. I crave that more than designer packages wrapped up in self-importance. I desire someone who is kind, genuine and warm. Someone who cares and isn't affected by status and position. A woman who has suffered through no fault of her own and is still a pure soul. I desire all that in you, baby, because you are everything I'm searching for and everything I *don't* deserve. You see…"

He brushes his lips against mine and whispers, "I'm not a nice man, as it happens. I kill, torture, and break men for a living. I search out their weakness and use it against them. I back up a demon and cover his tracks. I intimidate, threaten, and thrive on other people's misery, and I feed off the souls of good people to make myself feel better. All my life, I've hated the raw evil that surrounds me. I've seen terrible things that would send the sanest person mad within seconds. I'm not proud of who I am. I am the lowest form of life, but I learned a long time ago I can't change that. Not really."

I open my mouth to speak and his own descends on it with a punishing, brutal kiss that leaves me reeling. Flynn's passion is fierce, devastating, and relentless and he kisses me with all the intensity of a desperate man. His fingers clutch my hair and press me closer, and his low moan of passion excites me in a way I wasn't expecting.

He pulls back and rests his head against mine and says in a rough voice, "I need a woman like you in my life, Louisa, to neutralize the anger. To bring me back from the edge and reassure me that everything will be ok. I need you way more than you need me, and I will worship every inch of you for sticking by my side. I find you the most attractive woman I have ever seen and there is not a minute of the day I don't desire you. You say you are unattractive; I disagree. I have never met a more attractive woman in my life and if you allow it, I want to prove that and make you happier than you have ever been. I don't need your money. I don't care what clothes you wear. I'm not interested in how many pounds you carry, it's just more of you to love. If you don't wear make-up, that means nothing to me because when I look at you, I see everything I ever wanted. So, push away those doubts and embrace the power you have because I have never met anyone as impressive as you, Louisa Sullivan, and don't let anyone tell you differently."

Just like that, the worries disappear like smoke to the heavens. It carries away any self-doubt I had and replaces it with an energy that's new and exciting. I finally understand what it's like. To be desired, important even, and not on my own anymore and I would do anything for this man because he has stepped inside my soul and breathed life into my frozen heart. As the warmth and energy spreads through my body, I feel so different. As if I'm invincible and it's because of him. Flynn Vasquez, the dark angel who walked into my life and turned it upside down. With him beside me, I can do anything, and he has given me the confidence to face the world and raise my middle finger knowing I am loved.

CHAPTER 22

FLYNN

I am so angry. Iris Young just confirmed what I have always known. I wasn't loved and never wanted. The only person who did was told I had died. They will wish I had. Wesley Vasquez used me to prolong his own miserable life. Used his own son as a bargaining chip to ensure the protection of the biggest bastard I have ever heard of. He tortured me on repeat for fun, knowing I was the product of his sick and twisted mind and death will be too good for him when I get my revenge.

As we walk to the elevator, so many thoughts are twisting my emotions into a dark picture of revenge. So much is swirling around me like a dark cloak of destruction. I am going to make them all pay, and it won't be pretty. Their sins will catch up with them and I thank God I never killed Wesley before this day because his death will be a long, slow, and painful one.

I am known as the mad one. The one with chaos as his middle name. Maybe now it's time to let the madness take over and discover what I'm capable of.

Louisa is silent as she regards me with concern and

somehow through all the darkness, the savage madness that this day has delivered is the one thing that has me clinging to sanity. Her. The woman who is my light in the darkness. She brings me home and makes everything better and I am already a better person with her in my life. Now I just need to let her know that.

The silence hovers between us in the elevator and I can tell she's nervous. There's a flush to her cheeks and an excitement in her eyes that tells me I need to make this count. I know she's a virgin. It's obvious by the slightly nervous look in her eyes and the embarrassment on her face. She's scared of something she knows nothing about and it's my job to chase away those self-doubts and make this an experience she will always treasure.

As the elevator arrives at our destination, we walk into the penthouse and she says nervously, "Um, shall I order up lunch?"

I can tell she's doing everything possible to delay the inevitable because I'm guessing she's nervous and despite the hell I have fallen into, there is only one thing on my mind. Loving her.

"Louisa."

My husky whisper makes her stop and look up nervously. "Yes, Flynn?"

"Come here."

The pink tinge to her cheeks makes me smile as she shuffles nervously toward me. As she stands before me, a quivering mass of doubts, I reach out and trace a soft path down her face and whisper, "Close your eyes."

She does as I ask and as I brush my lips to hers, I whisper, "What can you see?"

"I don't understand." Her voice is breathless, needy even and I laugh softly, "What do you see standing behind your eyes?"

She doesn't falter. "You."

"What do you want?"

"You." She doesn't hesitate and I gently stroke her face, loving how she shivers.

"You do know it will change everything."

"How?"

Her eyes flicker and I say firmly, "Keep them closed."

Then I briefly brush my lips against hers and whisper, "Because once I claim your innocence, you will always be mine. I won't let you go. Now, what do you see standing behind your eyes?"

Gently, I kiss her neck and her voice trembles. "You, Flynn, only you."

"And what are you thinking right now?"

"That I..." she falters, and I bite down gently on her neck, making her groan. "I want you to get rid of my fucking virginity, Flynn, and show me how good it can be."

Laughing softly against her neck, I say in a husky voice, "And you understand the consequences. That you will be mine and I will own you."

Her eyelids flicker and I say firmly, "Keep them closed."

I love her sass as she says, "Like fuck will you own me." Laughing to myself, I growl, "That's where you're wrong, baby. Once I take you, I will crawl so deep inside I will leave with your heart. I will blow your mind from the inside and take no prisoners. You will belong to me in every way, and you will never want it any different. You see, Louisa, this is it for me. I have met the woman I want more than anything and you think owning someone is a bad thing, it's not. I forgot to mention that by agreeing to this, you already own my heart and only one other person in my miserable life has that honor."

Her eyes flick open, and I hate the hurt in them as she whispers, "Who was she?"

The pain returns and I say roughly, "My nanny."

Her eyes soften and she says in her lilting, gentle voice, "What happened to her?"

Shaking my head, I place my finger on her lips and smile. "That's a story for another day. Not now. Not in this moment. This is *our* moment, Louisa. This is the one when we become lovers, and nothing else matters than that."

"Lovers." Her eyes widen and I nod firmly. "If you agree, that is."

Her breathing is erratic, and her eyes shine with desire, and I have never seen a more beautiful sight. In fact, I just stare at a goddess in all her natural beauty and watch her chest heave and her pupils dilate as she says huskily, "I want you, Flynn. I want it to be you and you already own me."

Stepping forward, I can wait no more and as I take her hand and lead her to the bedroom, I feel a peace I never expected.

CHAPTER 23

LOUISA

This is it. I know it's going to happen and I'm impatient for that. I'm not even embarrassed, which surprises me. The doubts have been erased and, if anything, I can't wait.

For him.

To experience what it's like to be loved. I really believe he is genuine. Nobody could fake emotion like that. Flynn is like a blank page with a mirror into his soul. So closed and enigmatic one moment and then when he allows it, the drapes part and I see the emotion inside. He is an enigma; a complicated man of extremes and I still can't believe I got so lucky. I know he's not a catch in the usual sense of the word. A bad man, he says. A killer and cold-blooded murderer and a man with no shame. Not exactly the man your father intended for your future, but love has a strange habit of rewriting the rules.

As we enter the guest bedroom, I hold my breath as Flynn stands and removes his shirt and shrugs out of his pants. I'm not surprised to see he has nothing on underneath, and I try hard not to stare at something that is already making my eyes water.

His soft voice drifts toward me as he says, "Take off your clothes."

"I can't." I whisper with shame and embarrassment and just wish he would draw the drapes and let the darkness hide my body from his eager eyes.

"Louisa, take off your clothes."

His voice is firm and with a sigh, I reach for my top and my hands tremble as I pull it over my head. I have never stood before a man in my underwear before and his gentle voice says, "Now your skirt."

The shame washes over me as I step out of my skirt and hate that my unattractive underwear must be seriously turning him off right now. A lone tear escapes as I struggle with what he's asking and then, to my surprise, a gentle finger brushes it away and he whispers, "You are so beautiful."

"I'm..."

"Beautiful." His voice is firm and offers no argument and he twists my hair around his fingers and whispers, "You are an angel. A beautiful angel who doesn't realize how powerful she is. Look at me, Louisa."

I flutter my eyes open and see pure lust looking back at me, and he growls like a tortured soul. "I want you more than I have wanted any other woman in my life. I am holding everything I ever wanted in my arms, and I won't let you feel ashamed of that."

"I'm not ashamed of you, Flynn."

His mouth silences my words and as he kisses me deeply, I sense the anguish being chipped away one kiss at a time.

His hands slide around my back and unhook my bra and as it falls to the ground, his low moan of desire does something to me inside. He bends his lips to capture my nipple between his teeth, causing me to gasp out loud and as he sucks on my breast, it's like nothing on earth. His other hand moves lower and rips off my panties, and to my complete mortification, he kneels before me and buries his face against my throbbing pussy.

His tongue sweeps along the length of it, causing me to groan and as the wet trail welcomes him inside, he gently parts my thighs and sucks and tastes my clit, causing me to cry out.

This is the most exquisite torture and suddenly nothing else matters but the pleasure he is inflicting on my body.

The licking, biting, and tasting causes his own groans to join mine. It makes me bolder, and I twist my fingers in his hair and as he stands and pulls me flush against his body, I love how good it is.

It gives me courage to explore his own body and I love how he groans when I lick and bite his own flesh, dropping onto my knees to worship him as he did to me. I don't even hesitate and sweep my tongue around his crown and savor the drops that spill from the top. He fists my hair and guides my mouth onto the length of him and as he slides inside, he fills me completely with his shaft that lies like velvet against my tongue. As he eases back and forth, I suck and lick and am empowered by his response to that. His heavy breathing and low moans spur me on when I see what I can do for him.

He thrusts deeper into the back of my throat and it's as if he fills me entirely. Then he pulls out and drags me roughly to my feet and the lust blazing from his eyes turns me on way more than I ever thought it would. It's suddenly so incredibly important to feel him inside me and my pussy is throbbing with an urgent need that shocks me a little. He leads me across to the bed and pushes me gently back and I'm not ashamed as he stands staring at the whole of me while I lie back against the sheets.

"You are so beautiful, Louisa. I can't believe I got so lucky."

His compliment makes me sexy, desirable and loved and when he growls low in his throat, "Spread your legs," I'm not even ashamed to do as he asks.

Dropping to his knees, he buries his face against my wet heat and licks and bites until the sensation is almost unbearable. I'm surprised to find it's not enough and I want so much more and as he crawls up my body, worshipping every inch of it, he settles between my thighs and whispers, "Taste how much your body wants me."

As he kisses me deeply, I am aroused by the flavor of my virtue on his tongue and as he pushes against my opening with his hard cock, I am considering begging him to fuck me and not to stop. Instead, he hesitates and strokes my hair lovingly and whispers, "I'll grab a condom and then, if you are happy to continue, I want to fuck you all night long."

His dirty words are like a pin from a grenade, and I say breathlessly, "Fuck the condom, Flynn. I don't want anything between us."

"But..."

"I'm on the pill and clean and I don't need a medical certificate from you either, because for some irrational reason, I trust you."

He stares at me with such an expression of love I hitch my breath because as moments go, this one is the best of my life and he says huskily, "I'm clean. I have never been inside any woman unprotected, so this is a first for me."

He gazes in wonder into my eyes and as he eases in, there is a sharp pain as he pushes through my last defense. I call out but he captures it in his mouth and as his large cock grazes my walls, I'm so full it's as if he has crawled into my body and, as he said, owns it.

With his skin flush against mine and his breathing heavy against my cheek, I'm surprised by how natural this is. Just knowing he is inside me turns me on way more than I ever thought it would and as he cups my ass and pulls me even closer, I enjoy a glorious sense of fulfillment.

He thrusts deeper, faster, harder, and my mind is scrambled

as it struggles to deal with the emotions and sensations he is creating. It's like a lethal cocktail as he intoxicates my senses and as he powers through my final defense, I cry out as his cock pushes against my clit, rubbing it, stimulating it, and owning it. Time has no meaning now. I don't even register where we are, just the building wave of euphoria that he has created. An urgency for something unknown fills me as I hold my breath and then with one final thrust a sensation so glorious races through my body like a river that's burst its banks and as my body shudders and convulses under his, he roars against me as his own climax spills deep inside my womb.

CHAPTER 24

FLYNN

Unprotected sex is the best kind of sex. When I experienced my woman as nature intended, it caused a possessive streak to fire through my body and explode with a huge resolve to love her forever. I knew Louisa was everything I had been searching for from the moment we met. The fact she was chosen for me on paper and by circumstance is irrelevant now. None of that matters because she was always my woman. I just never knew it.

As we lie wrapped in sweat, semen, and blood, I couldn't give a fuck. I want every part of her and as I drop light kisses on her breasts and inhale the scent of my sex on her body, a protective shield wraps itself around my heart.

She trembles against me as I say softly, "Does it hurt, baby?"

"A little." She sounds shy and yet so happy it brings a smile to my face and I lean back and gaze at her with the adoration she deserves, whispering, "Thank you."

"For what?" She grins shyly and I brush my lips against hers and murmur, "For allowing me to be the one."

The tears glisten in her eyes and as I fall to the side, I drag her with me, and she rests her cheek on my chest as I play with her luxurious hair.

"Was it ok?" Her voice sounds anxious, and I smile to myself. "More than ok, baby, that fucking blew my mind."

She giggles and hearing it makes me happier than I thought it would and she says tentatively, "You don't have to say anything, but what happened to your nanny?"

I'm waiting for the pain to stir up the madness, but instead all I'm hit with is a great wave of sadness that has been diluted by the happiness I hold in my heart right now. With Louisa in my arms, now may be the perfect time to purge my soul of the one demon that hurts me more than anything.

"You won't like it, baby." I say with a sigh. "Maybe another time."

I give her the option to back out because this is a story that never leaves your memory. It stars in your nightmares and lives with you throughout the day and Louisa doesn't deserve to have those images in her mind.

"I want to know." She sounds annoyed, fierce even, and it makes me smile to think of the strong woman lying in my arms. She is always so curious, and I love that about her. Nothing is off limits and so for the first time in my life, I prepare to open Pandora's box.

"Her name was Rosemary." Just hearing her name spoken out loud drives the perpetual knife deeper, and I sigh. Louisa plants a soft kiss in my chest and whispers, "It's ok, Flynn."

It gives me the courage to see this through and I say in almost a whisper, "She was my nanny and the only person who was ever kind to me, and I must have been only seven when she…"

I break off and shift my emotions in place because this story is one I will never forget.

"Wesley was packing me off to school and a few days before I was due to leave, he burst into the nursery and stood there with a twisted expression on his face. He said we had no use for her anymore and it confused me. It was obvious Rosemary hated him. I always sensed that from the hatred in her eyes when he hung around, and I'm guessing it's because of the way he treated us both."

"Both?"

Louisa's question makes me sigh. "I got used to the beatings, the sharp words, and the constant imprisonment. If I did anything to upset him, he would shove me in a cupboard, sometimes for hours, with no food or water. Rosemary was always the one to comfort me and reassure me that everything would be ok. She chased the shadows away and told me stories of happy times and a future that would be mine if I worked hard and kept a kind soul. She was the only good thing in my life and when he told me she was no longer required, it filled me with so much pain and fear and it must have shown because he slapped me hard across the face and told me to man up."

"Bastard." Louisa's disgusted voice makes me laugh and my breath hitches as I revisit my darkest hour.

"The night before I left for school, he threw a party. We heard the noise from the top of the house where we both lived. Louisa held me and rocked me gently, promising to write and stay in touch. She would visit me and never leave me. She would always be there and if I ever needed anything, to call her. It helped knowing I had someone who loved me. Someone to count on and then Wesley appeared, and it was obvious he had been drinking. He had that wild edge in his eyes I had seen many times before and he ordered us to go downstairs and say our goodbyes."

"I fucking hate that bastard. What a waste of life he is."

Louisa growls with anger and I couldn't agree more.

"Rosemary tried to act as if everything was ok. She took my hand and squeezed it and as we followed him to the party, I remember being so frightened. The room was full of men like him. His soldiers, associates, and people that scared me to death. Rosemary must have been so afraid, but she never once showed it. She smiled her reassurance and tried to make me relax. I remember Wesley announcing us to the room and insulting her. He called her a fat slag and laughed that no man would ever be seen dead with a woman like her. It confused me. I didn't understand what he meant and thought it was cruel, then again, he always was."

I break off and the rage fires up my blood as I hiss, "He dragged her away from me into the middle of the room. I made to follow her, and another man pulled my arms behind my back and held me as Wesley screeched, let the boy see how we deal with trashy women like this."

Louisa tenses and I stroke her hair absentmindedly.

"He ripped off her clothes and as she stood naked in the room, his guests jeered and called her horrible names. She smiled at me the whole time as if everything was fine. But I feared for her and even at that age I sensed something bad was going to happen and as Wesley pushed her back onto the table, he raped her in front of the whole fucking room."

Louisa sobs and I stroke her back absentmindedly, too far gone to offer her any comfort.

"I remember staring into her eyes the entire time as she smiled at me as if this was ok and as every last man in that room took his turn, I was forced to watch. After they finished Wesley came to me and laughed in my face and told me that was all women were good for and she had loved every minute of it. To take notes and treat every woman this way because only a real man made the grade. Then he turned back to her and laughed, and I watched in horror as she lay there with blood tricking between her thighs. She had scratches and cuts all over her body, and the bruises were already changing the color of her skin. Wesley announced to the room that he was regrettably going to have to fire the nanny, and everyone laughed when he took out his gun and placed the barrel in her mouth. Even then she looked at me with so much love in her eyes and as he pulled the trigger, my life ended with hers."

Saying the words out loud tears my soul apart and Louisa's soft kisses on my chest hold me back from falling into the madness. As she strokes my skin, she whispers, "I can't begin to imagine how you are feeling, Flynn, but you are not on your own anymore. You have me and I will never leave you. Together, we will bring your uncle down and you will be free. Nothing will ever come between us; you have my word on that."

Just hearing those words is enough and as I kiss my woman, I know she sits beside the angel who has always lived in my heart. The most beautiful woman from my past who didn't deserve to be cut down and murdered in cold blood, right before my eyes. She was told she was ugly, trash, and undesirable. But she was beautiful to me. She had a golden heart, and it shone through the packaging and made her a goddess. They are the women that attract me the most. The women that cast everyone else in their shade. I have found my own piece of perfection in Louisa, and I will make it my life's work to make hers a happy one.

CHAPTER 25

LOUISA

I'm so worried about Flynn. When he told me about Rosemary, I was broken. I tried so hard to be strong but imagining his life and what he had to witness explains everything. It's almost certain we will have a fight on our hands to be together, but if I lose everything but him, I will consider myself richer for it.

After his story ended, we made love again. This time it was with a firm resolve attached. As lovers, partners and forging a bond that nothing will ever break. Out of tragedy, a fierce, protective love has formed and understanding his past will help our future.

"I don't want to go home." I groan as we pack our bags and wait for the cab to take us to the airfield.

"We must, baby. We have much to do before we can move on from this."

Flynn kisses me gently and I'm fearful of what lies ahead.

I know that he asked a friend of his to trace Massimo's daughter. He sent the text after our meeting with Iris Young, and I'm curious about that.

"What will you do if you find Massimo's daughter?"

Flynn laughs softly. "I will do nothing, my angel. It's out of my hands now."

"Then whose hands is it in?"

Flynn merely grins, and I watch the excitement flare in his eyes.

"Someone who will know exactly what to do."

The phone rings announcing our cab has arrived and as we bid farewell to the penthouse, I'm sad that our cozy bubble is about to burst.

"What will we tell my father?"

I'm nervous about that and as Flynn rests his arms around my shoulder, he says reassuringly, "We will tell him everything. He has a right to that, at least."

"Everything!" The blood drains from my face and Flynn laughs. "Well, maybe not absolutely everything, just what we need him to know."

He drops a light kiss on the top of my head and sighs. "I'm guessing he won't be happy about us. I wouldn't be if you were my daughter."

"Why not? He couldn't have found a more suitable, well, um, suitor if he tried."

I giggle and he twists his fingers in mine and raises them to his lips. "Well, obviously we know that, but well, he will be afraid for you. My world is dark and extreme and there is no place in it for a woman like you."

Now I'm fearful and my voice shakes. "What do you mean?"

"It means I will do everything to keep you safe."

I'm uneasy because there is so much against us and now that I've found Flynn, I'm waiting for fate to whisk him away again as quickly.

We reach the airfield and my heart sinks. In a few hours' time, we will be home and things may change. Flynn has business to attend to and so do I. Just thinking about going back to work with all this happening around me makes my head hurt. I want to remain by Flynn's side and guide him through it but understand it will help him more if I stay out of his business.

"What are you thinking?"

He drops a light kiss on my lips, and I smile brightly. "That I don't want to go back to work."

He looks into my eyes and smiles. "It may be what you need to distract you from this madness."

"Or add to it."

I groan out loud. "Why did my father partner me up with that creep? I was loving life before that and now I'm dreading going to the office."

"Then prove you're better than him. You already are, so it won't be difficult."

I smile at him with so much love, my heart aches under the strain. "You make me feel better about myself, Flynn. That's some gift you have there."

"It's easy when it concerns you."

As we make the journey home, it's the sweetest yet the most desperate. When we land, it will signify a new beginning, at least I'm hopeful for that and not the ending I fear when my father learns exactly how close I've got to his stepson.

* * *

Vivian's smiling face is the first thing that greets us when we head through the door, and I don't miss the hunger in her gaze as she looks at her son. He is happy to see her. It's obvious from the softening of his eyes and the smile he directs her way as she pulls him into her arms.

After learning what a terrible life he has had up until now, it makes my heart glow and I wonder how I'll feel if I'm made to walk away so that Vivian can have a relationship with her son. On the one hand, I think my father will understand, but on the other, he may be angry and tell us it's one or the other.

I'm not sure how things will pan out and I'm nervous about that.

"Where's dad?" I interrupt their homecoming, and Vivian looks up and smiles. "He won't be long; he's taking a call in the den."

Almost on cue, we hear a deep voice, "Sorry guys, business never goes away."

I turn and a wave of love hits me for my father. The pleasure in his eyes as he holds out his arms has me running into them as if I am ten years old again. As they wrap around me, I squeeze my eyes tightly against the tears and love how secure he always makes me feel.

"How did it go?" He's referring to the business I pretended I was there for, and I'm a little guilty about that and with a sinking heart I decide he deserves the truth, so I say softly, "Daddy, we have something to tell you."

The tension increases in the room as I watch my father exchange a look with Vivian, who appears anxious and I nod reassuringly to Flynn and say, "Perhaps we should all go into the living room and grab a drink. I'm guessing we'll need one when Flynn finishes his story."

We share a smile, and it doesn't go unnoticed as the realization dawns in Vivian's eyes. I hate the anxious expression that replaces the happy one and hope they can move past our family connection and understand we aren't related by blood and there is nothing wrong with this.

Flynn smiles at his mother and I see a softening in her features and if anyone can persuade them, he can, so as we all head to the living room for the showdown I always knew was coming, I wonder what state our relationships will be in when we walk out of there.

CHAPTER 26

FLYNN

I don't get nervous—ever. I don't entertain fear and always face my problems head on with a cool detachment. But the anxiety on the faces of the two women who mean the most to me in the world is making me nervous. I don't want to upset either one of them, but this tale could blow their worlds apart.

The resignation in Dimitri's eyes tells me he knows already, and I'm not surprised about that because Louisa looks ten shades different to when she left. There's a happiness in her face that reflects her beauty and it's as if someone has colored in the edges and she radiates happiness. Vivian also looks resigned to it and so, like the best diversion tactic, I dive straight in and tell them what happened with Iris Young.

Vivian looks at me with tears pouring from her eyes and whispers, "I'm so sorry, Flynn."

"I'm not." I shrug. "It was the best possible outcome because now I'm in no way related to Massimo Delauren."

Dimitri looks sharply at Louisa, and I can see him connecting the dots in his mind and with a sigh of resignation, he fixes me with a knowing look. "Then I guess things will change around here."

"Why?" Vivian speaks out and I hear the anxiety in her voice, making him smile reassuringly. "I'm not blind, Vivian. My daughter left here with a very different expression on her face and has returned positively blooming. I'm guessing your son has a lot to do with that, which presents us with a huge problem."

Vivian looks down and, to my surprise, is trying to disguise a smile.

I glance at Louisa, who is looking so anxious I want to drag her beside me and reassure her that everything will be ok and Dimitri sighs heavily. "So, Flynn, what exactly are your intentions toward my daughter?"

I'm impressed at his direct question and respect him even more for it. Louisa looks as if she wants to disappear in a puff of smoke and it's almost amusing to see the embarrassment written all over her face.

"Sir, I would like permission to date your daughter."

I lay it straight out there because I'm guessing Dimitri would prefer it that way and the room falls silent as we wait for his answer to that.

He looks at Louisa and then at Vivian and I hate the uncertainty in his eyes. So, before he can speak, I say quickly, "It's true, this situation isn't perfect and I'm probably the last man on earth you want in your daughter's life. I live a hard life surrounded by violence that promises to get even worse before it gets better. I have nothing to offer except my love and devotion and having just found my family, I'm aware that I'm already testing that. But then I met your daughter and nothing else seemed to matter."

I smile at Louisa and love the light shining from her eyes as she stares at me with support written all over her face. Turning to Vivian, I say gently, "The last thing I want is to upset you.

Above everything I want you in my life and to build a relationship. There is so much to talk of and learn about one another, but I can't help the strong feelings I have for your stepdaughter. I wasn't expecting that and if I'm honest, which is what I will always be, is that initially I came here for her."

They all stare at me in stunned surprise, and I lean back and sigh heavily. "The most important thing in my life is to destroy Massimo. He controls all our lives and carries out his reign of terror in the cruelest of ways. He has taken a woman my friends and I care deeply about, and I'm certain he is making her life a living hell."

Louisa appears as if she's about to faint and Vivian seems concerned as she shares a strained look with her husband. I'm sure Louisa will be thinking I'm just like everyone else and I say gently, "Winter is my friend's sister, his twin sister. We all attended college together and before that ended, she was kidnapped and forced to marry Massimo. He keeps her well-guarded and has molded her into his perfect shadow. It's as if her humanity has been stripped from her soul and it's vital we bring her back to us. The plan was to marry for power. Gather an army who would protect us from Massimo and his formidable family and bring Winter home. Initially, that was my plan when I learned who you were, sir, and hoped to harness the hatred you have for your brother to help our plan."

Louisa gasps and looks so destroyed it bruises my soul.

Turning to her, I say with unexpected emotion. "Then I met you, Louisa and it wouldn't have mattered if I came here for a different reason entirely. There was something about you that hit me hard. It was as if I was seeing my destiny and to learn we could be related destroyed me in a way I never saw coming. The reason I came here was no longer important. The most important thing was to prove we weren't related and not for the reasons you think."

You could cut the tension in the room with a knife as I say

sadly, "All my life I wished for a family. I used to imagine what that would feel like. I would look around at people who had loving ones and envy them their happiness. My whole life has been filled with pain. Physical and mental torture, and the first person who showed me a different way was Winter. She was kind, loving, and easy to be around. We all fell in love with her at Rockwell Academy, as we became a family of sorts. She showed me something I wanted for myself. The importance of family and when I first set eyes on Louisa, I wanted mine with her."

Vivian can't stop the tears from spilling down her face and I feel bad for that and smile at her with sadness. "There is everything I want in this room, and yet you probably wish it was different. I may have come here with questions and a hidden agenda, but I want to be open and honest about that and tell you that agenda may remain, but my feelings shifted direction. I will do everything I can to make Louisa happy, sir."

I stare directly at Dimitri, whose face is like thunder, and then I turn to Louisa and say with a slight break in my voice. "I'm not here for your inheritance, your connections, or your family. I came here to find my mother and in doing so, I found a woman I will love for eternity if I'm allowed."

Louisa frantically wipes the tears from her eyes and Vivian says shakily, "It changes nothing for me, Flynn. You are still my son, and I will always stand beside you. If Dimitri thinks different, I will respect his opinion, but I will always have a relationship with you, Flynn, whatever happens here today. It's taken me so long to find you and I will never let you go."

My heart sags in relief and Louisa says sharply, "I may not like hearing the reasons you came, but I can tell you speak from the heart. I want to see where our road leads, Flynn and if my father can't give us his blessing, then we will deal with that, but we'll do it together."

I love the fierce determination in her face and as Dimitri speaks, we look at him in combined shock as he says loudly, "Oh, for fuck's sake, why is life so complicated?"

He shakes his head and says sternly, "Whatever your reasons for coming here don't matter now. We will deal with the situation as it is, and we have a huge problem."

I hold my breath as he growls. "My fucking brother is a monster, a sadist, and a bastard and that has never been any different. I tried to bring him down once and, like the cockroach he is, he just shook himself off and reinforced his empire. No, I am with you on this, and I know a man who can help us. And Louisa…"

His face softens, and he says with a weariness in his voice, "Even I can see you've changed. There's a happiness in you that's different, and I'm guessing love has a lot to do with that. I'm not happy about the situation, but I'm not stupid enough to start laying down ultimatums. The fact you're not related takes away the main obstacle for me and if I'm to guarantee your safety, we need to cut off the snake's head. Flynn may live in a violent world, but I can tell he has a good heart and I'm counting on him proving me right about that, so this is what we will do."

He glares around the room with a fierce protective expression on his face and growls, "We pay Pedro a visit and I'm guessing he will be only too happy to assist us in this matter. There is only one other person who detests my brother as much as I do, and he will take great pleasure in helping you in any way he can."

I stare at Louisa's father with overwhelming respect and can't believe how well he has taken this. I'm in awe of him and it appears his wife and daughter are too, which shows me immediately how he has grown so successful. It takes a strong man to roll with the punches and Dimitri is obviously a professional, so with a great sense of relief and hope for the future, I take the glass of champagne he offers me and toast a very different future to the one I thought I had.

CHAPTER 27

LOUISA

I'm surprised at how well my father has taken this and when the champagne bottle is empty, Vivian and Flynn head to the kitchen to make coffee and I guess it's just an opportunity for them to talk. I feel a little nervous as I sit with my father and wonder what's running through his mind right now.

"Louisa." The soft tone of his voice makes me glance up in surprise and he pats the seat beside him.

"Come here, honey. I have something to tell you."

I swear my heart thumps so hard he can hear it, and as I do as he says, I'm surprised when he takes my hand and sighs. "I'm not going to pretend I'm ecstatic about this, but there is only one thing that concerns me."

I feel a little on edge as he says softly, "You."

"Me?"

He nods. "When your mother died, I was so afraid for you. I hated that you would grow up never really knowing how strong she was. How amazing and how wise and all of this..." He waves his hand around the room. "Was because of her. She picked me up when I was down and placed me back on track.

She was the rock I needed and my best friend. I don't think she was afraid of anything, and I see a lot of her in you."

He places his arm around my shoulders and pulls me tight against him, and it's as if I'm ten years old again.

"I watched you struggle when Crystal came into our lives. She wasn't half the person your own mother was and yet you tried so hard to welcome her. I understood the yearning you had for a normal family, and I would have done anything to give that to you. When Sienna came along, I was happy you had a sister. You weren't on your own anymore, and I hoped you'd be friends."

He laughs ruefully. "I never really expected you to be so different. However, despite her flaws, I know Sienna loves you. She doesn't show it in the best of ways, but I see it in her eyes. She needs a little more guidance and I'm guessing will marry some schmuck from the valley, but if that's what makes her happy, then I can't ask for more."

I swallow hard because my father has never opened up to me like this and it's surprising me.

"I was never worried about Sienna's future quite as much as yours."

He sighs heavily and squeezes my shoulder. "You are so like your mother. You have strong opinions and don't tolerate fools easily. I watched you have a hard time compared to Sienna and knew that you would only marry for love. It worried me that you would rather be alone than tolerate any of the guys who came calling and I'm ashamed to admit that I paired you up with Brad in the hope you would grow closer to him."

"You did that?" I'm incensed, and he laughs out loud. "Of course, I did. I thought if I put you two together, you would grow to like him. He is driven, good at business, a little cocky, but I was certain you could deal with that, and I had hoped you would realize you were perfect for one another. I never factored in Flynn Vasquez, though, and I saw the looks you shared before the weekend and I'm not stupid. I guessed the meetings were an excuse to spend time with him. I'm not a fool, Louisa. I can tell when I'm being played, and you weren't as subtle as you think you were."

This time I laugh out loud and for a second, we share a moment that's so special I wish it was possible to box it up forever. I love my dad; I always have, and his approval means the world to me.

Then he sighs and pulls me harder against him. "It won't be easy, though."

"I know."

I'm under no illusions about that and ask the burning question on my lips, "Why are you helping him bring your brother down? There must be another reason because it's not on my behalf."

Once again, he laughs softly. "You're sharp, Louisa, and you always have been. No…"

He says angrily, "It's for Vivian. That bastard Wesley ruined her. He damaged her physically, mentally, and ripped out her heart when he stole her son. If I bring Massimo down, I bring him down too and one thing is guaranteed, Wesley will not survive this if I have to pull the trigger myself."

I'm surprised at the venom in his voice and the anger that surrounds him like a destructive force, and he growls, "We need a man like Flynn. Strong, unafraid, but with his soul edged with honor. He's far from perfect, but that's through no fault of his own. I recognize a good man when I see one and he has given me no reason to doubt that opinion I have of him. I see a lot of Vivian in him and not just in his appearance, but I understand those people, honey. Your uncle is one of them. My own family was from the same mold and it runs through my blood too. I may be a respectable businessman now, but inside I am every bit as ruthless. I chose a different life because I could. Flynn is working with what he has, and I can tell he's got a good heart. You will be the best part of him, like your mother was with me and how would I not give my blessing based on that alone?"

"I love you, daddy." I hug him so hard he chuckles.

"I love you too, honey."

We look up as Vivian heads into the room with Flynn close behind, carrying a tray of coffee. I don't miss his anxious expression and I smile, loving how his eyes pull me in and hold my heart hostage all over again.

Jumping up, I head across and take the tray from him and smile happily, loving the relief on his face as he turns to my father.

"Thank you, sir."

"Thank me when we rid the world of Wesley Vasquez and his best friend."

I hand a coffee to my father and watch his arm fall around Vivian's shoulder as she takes my place and snuggles into his side. As I sit beside Flynn, I take his hand and the love in his eyes makes me so happy I almost pinch myself. I never really expected a moment like this. I hoped for a moment like this all my life and never believed it would happen. But it has and now it's the most important thing in the world to make it count and move on as a family and set Winter free because in achieving that, the chains fall from every last one of us who have been affected by Massimo Delauren and Wesley Vasquez.

CHAPTER 28

FLYNN

Pedro Carlos is a man I'm familiar with. I understand his life because I live one the same.

We touch down in Colombia and the blacked-out windows of the cars that stand waiting for us wraps me in familiarity. Mafia comes in many forms and Pedro Carlos is the best at what he does in Colombia.

Today we flew with two extra passengers. A family visit or a business one. Both, I suppose, and as we take our seats in the two waiting cars, I know Pedro favors caution above everything.

Louisa snuggles by my side and whispers, "Why aren't we traveling with my father and Vivian?"

"Security, baby."

I drop a kiss on her lips and grin. "Your uncle knows the score. If we are ambushed, we stand a better chance apart. One car may survive, which limits the casualties."

"You're kidding me." Louisa appears anxious and I shrug. "It's our world and you will get used to it."

She grips my hand, and I don't think I will ever stop desiring this woman. Out of respect to our family, we slept apart last night, but there won't be many more of them. I need Louisa by my side as if she is one of my own limbs and I am surprised how quickly I reached that point. I have always been alone. I preferred it, but when she came into my life, I found an overwhelming need to keep her by my side. It's as if I can't breathe unless she is safe and she will never be safer than by my side. If I'm anxious about anything, it's that any harm will come to her because of me and that is why I'm not stopping until every threat is dealt with and we can breathe a huge sigh of relief.

I am used to amazing homes. My own is a fortress and Dimitri lives like a King. Pedro, it seems likes to flaunt his wealth and I smirk to myself when we pass through huge, pillared gates with a gold crown on each stone column. The ornamental gardens stretch along the sweeping driveway and the white house that appears around the bend almost sparkles in the sunlight. I'm not sure where it ends because I've never seen a house as big as this in my life. It has no end and I'm certain could contain a small town within its walls.

"Your uncle likes the finer things in life, it seems." I can't help saying.

Louisa laughs. "He's a little ostentatious with his money, but you'll like him. He's a teddy bear."

Biting back a grin, I'm guessing he is anything but. More like a grizzly bear with sharp claws because his reputation precedes him. Pedro Carlos is a man even I wouldn't like to meet on a dark night. He cuts his enemies down before they can even make an excuse and disposes of their assets in a damaging way. Unlike Massimo, though, he doesn't torture for fun and has a strict moral code where it concerns his family. His own live a respectable life and he has high expectations of them. His sons joined him in the family business along with his daughters, who, by all accounts, married well and provided him with several grandchildren, all of whom live in this giant fortress. A family man and a killer.

I'm interested to meet him.

* * *

As the cars come to a stop, the doors are wrenched open, and a surly guard looks inside and sweeps the cab with his eyes. As welcomes go, it's an unfriendly one, but I'm guessing security has no friends. They always expect the worst and act accordingly and only when he can see we mean no harm, does he nod and toss his eyes outside the car.

"Please stand facing the car."

He directs his words to me, and I catch the furious expression in Louisa's eyes as she opens her mouth to protest.

"It's ok, baby, the man's only doing his job."

I do as he says and as he searches me and removes my weapons, the flush on Louisa's face tells me that danger excites her. Wishing like crazy we were alone right now so I could take advantage of that, I wink and throw her a scorching look, promising we will revisit this moment when we are alone.

Dimitri and Vivian join us, and he says apologetically, "Sorry, Flynn, Pedro doesn't like surprises."

"It's fine. He's a wise man."

Loud laughter heads my way and as I turn, I see the man himself leaning against the huge front door, watching on with amusement.

"Uncle Pedro." Louisa breaks free and runs into his arms and the genuine warmth on his face at seeing her brings a smile to my lips.

"Mi Angel, you make me so happy."

He looks past her to Vivian and winks. "My beautiful Vivian, you bloom like a rare orchid in the desert."

Dimitri laughs out loud and rolls his eyes, taking his wife's hand firmly in his. "She is *my* rare bloom, Pedro, and don't you forget it."

I watch with interest as they embrace one another and feel the genuine warmth surrounding us.

This is what I crave. It's much the same when I meet up with my friends from Club Mafia, but aside from that, it's alien to me.

Louisa steps by my side and slips her hand in mine, causing Pedro to say with amusement, "It appears there are some questions to ask."

He frowns and Louisa rolls her eyes. "You go easy on Flynn, uncle. He doesn't need an interrogation."

I don't miss the steely glint in his eye as he looks between us and I'm guessing he has other ideas about that and as we follow him into the house, I prepare myself for a difficult visit ahead.

EVERYTHING I THOUGHT about Pedro Carlos is borne out as we wander through opulent rooms that are obviously the result of a well-run business. Drugs, extortion, arms, and other crimes are profitable because Pedro is the best at what he does. As his wife joins him, I'm not surprised to see she's young enough to be his daughter and is dripping in luxury. A tall willowy blonde with an amazing tan and figure and jewelry that probably cost millions of dollars, dangling from her neck and wrists.

A huge diamond ring flashes in the sunlight and as his arm slips around her waist, he says proudly, "Meet Sunny, wife number five."

I don't even want to know what happened to wives one to four and as everyone murmurs a polite greeting, my idea of the perfect family is distorted a little.

Dimitri and Vivian strike up a conversation with the couple

leaving me and Louisa standing by the open patio doors sipping the champagne Pedro insisted on.

"Wow, he doesn't hang around."

Louisa shakes her head as she looks at Sunny.

"What happened to wife number four?" I'm curious and Louisa grins. "Willow was a carbon copy of Summer. They don't last long because Pedro has a wandering eye. I believe Willow is currently enjoying her pay off in the arms of her fitness trainer."

"So, she's still alive?" I'm a little relieved about that and Louisa grins. "He's not a monster, just easily bored."

"Then I pity him because the best part I believe is the journey."

"Is that right?"

Louisa smiles so happily it takes all my self-control not to push her through those doors and lose us in this house for the entire afternoon.

For the most part, the day is spent catching up like any family occasion and we eat a fine lunch out on the terrace, surrounded by cooling fans under a gazebo. The wine flows and is obviously expensive and, like most families, the conversation is filled with jokes and laughter. When the final dish is cleared away, Pedro says easily, "Sunny, take Vivian and Louisa and show them the improvements you are making. I'm guessing they would be interested in that."

"Of course, baby boy, I would be happy to."

She stops and openly kisses Pedro with a deep, long lingering kiss that is quite embarrassing to watch. The fact her hand rests in his crotch makes me want to place my hands over Louisa's eyes because what the fuck, she's almost getting him off in full view of his guests.

Without warning he slaps her hard on the ass and as she yelps, he growls, "Later, baby girl."

She doesn't seem to mind and winks before saying in a

high-pitched voice, "Follow me girls. I can't wait to show you how generous my big bear is."

The expression on Louisa's face makes me wish for a camera right now and as they head off, I'm guessing she wishes she was anywhere else.

As soon as the women leave, the tension in the air increases and I see why Pedro is considered the biggest bastard in Colombia.

He turns his attention to me and snaps, "Why the fuck are you here?"

Dimitri looks at me apologetically and I maintain my blank expression and say evenly, "Because the two most important people in my life walked away from this table and I want to guarantee their safety."

"And you expect me to believe that?"

"It's the truth."

I stare him down and as testosterone collides in mid-air, Dimitri clears his throat. "Flynn has an interesting story to tell, Pedro, that I think you should listen to."

Still staring daggers at me, he growls, "I'm listening."

Without a hint of nerves, I relay the facts and watch his anger intensify with every word spoken. By the time I finish, I swear he's breathing fire, and he turns to Dimitri and growls, "That fucking bastard. How do you want me to end his life?"

"We need your help, not a hit."

"It would be my pleasure, my friend. Those bastards have lived too long already, and we are the idiots who allowed it."

"It's not that easy." Dimitri looks worried. "He has Flynn's friend and we both know he will guard her well. It won't be easy to set her free. Then there's Wesley. I'm guessing Massimo won't be so friendly when he learns what his closest friend did to him all those years ago. No, I've been thinking about this, and we have a golden opportunity to set them against one another and step back and watch the show."

"You think it's that easy?" Pedro spits on the ground. "I have no doubt Massimo will deal with Wesley. That will be the easy part but bringing *him* down is a different thing entirely."

Pedro looks thoughtful. "We need an enemy within."

My ears prick up and I say roughly, "Then you're looking at him."

Their eyes swing my way and I growl. "My entire life, I've been that enemy within my uncle's house. Watching and waiting for the opportune moment to rid me of him forever. If I must, I will do the same with Massimo. Gain his trust and bring him down inside his own walls."

I don't miss the look the two men share, which makes me strangely uneasy, and then Pedro leans forward and says in a disgusted voice. "The only way you will get inside Massimo's fortress is chained to his wall while he fucks you to death."

Dimitri looks sick and nods. "I'm sorry, Flynn, we've known for some time the details of my brother's perverted hobby. He takes young men and ruins them for fun and for all your skills, you will be exposed to that risk."

Pedro leans back and grabs his glass of whiskey, taking a long drag while wrestling with something on his mind.

"I have another idea that may work better. It will buy us some time and that is all, but will start the, how you say it, ball rolling."

"What do you have in mind?" I'm keen to hear the facts and he looks at Dimitri and smiles.

"We know something the great Massimo does not. His best friend betrayed him, and he has a daughter. Flynn will arrange a meeting with his uncle's best friend somewhere public, promising him his loyalty and, as a gift, he will deliver him a new toy to play with."

Dimitri looks worried. "How will that work?"

Pedro looks at me and, for the first time, I sense his acceptance and he smiles when I nod and say darkly, "I can do that."

Dimitri still looks confused, and I fix Pedro with a twisted smile. "The enemy within you say. I've been training for that role all my life. Leave it with me. I'll arrange everything and all I need to know is that I have your back up at my disposal when needed."

Pedro nods and then leans forward, staring me straight in the eye. "All the time you treat my Louisa properly, you have my loyalty. If you don't, you become my biggest enemy and I will end your life in the cruelest way possible. Do we have a deal?"

"We have a deal." I hold out my hand and as we shake on it, I see the promise in his eyes. I know he loves his goddaughter like one of his own and it's just a good thing I love her far more. He will be my ally until the end of time because I will never do anything to hurt Louisa and if I did, I would welcome death, anyway.

CHAPTER 29

LOUISA

Five minutes in and I'm ready to kill Sunny in cold blood. She chatters on about how much money Pedro spends on her and I want to pull my own ears off. As always, Vivian is polite and feigns interest, but I resist openly yawning. Luckily, as we make our way through their palatial home, a familiar face heads our way, holding the hand of a mini version of herself.

"Gloria." I open my arms and she beams broadly and heads into them. "Louisa, you are glowing, wait…"

She steps back and the knowing glint in her eyes makes me laugh out loud.

"I want to hear all about it." She turns to Sunny and says quickly, "I'm taking Louisa off your hands for a catch up. I hope you don't mind."

Sunny shakes her head and Vivian looks as if she would prefer to join us. "It's fine. You kids go and catch up. Vivian and I will enjoy a cozy chat while I show her how generous your father is."

As they head off, Gloria rolls her eyes. "She won't last long. She's annoying as fuck and even my father can't be that stupid."

"What happened to Polly? I always liked her." Polly was wife number three and Gloria sighs. "She was great. In fact, we are still in touch, but my father decided he fancied a change and that was it. I'm sure he regrets it now, but she went on to marry the chief of police."

We both laugh out loud, and Gloria grins. "I'm pretty sure he's still pumping her for information about my father."

We laugh even more and the little angel holding her mother's hand whines. "Mommy, I want to go swimming, you promised."

"Of course, my angel, I'll find Maria. She will go with you."

I follow them toward the open doors and as we step back out into the sunshine, I take a deep breath of pure oxygen. I've always loved coming here and spent many happy vacations in the company of Pedro's daughters, who were like sisters to me. Gloria in particular and as we settle down on the sunbeds, while Sophia runs to her nanny, who appears from out of nowhere, Gloria texts the maid to bring us a pitcher of lemonade and some cookies.

"This is nice. Are you here for long?"

She looks hopeful of that, and I sigh. "Only for the day. We need your father's help."

Gloria looks worried. "Are you in trouble?"

"Not me, but well, I should start at the beginning."

By the time I finish my story, Gloria's eyes are wide, and she looks worried. "My father will help, but are you sure this guy is genuine?"

As I think of Flynn, my expression softens, and she rolls her eyes. "For fuck's sake, I recognize that look. You're in love."

"I am."

I can't deny it and she grins, looking so pleased for me it makes me smile.

"I can't wait to meet him."

"He's a little different."

"In what way?"

"Mafia." I only need to say one word, and Gloria's eyes widen. "And you're happy with that?"

"Wait until you meet him."

I giggle and she shakes her head slowly. "But that won't be easy. Trust me, I know what it's like living under a threat your entire life."

Gloria married the son of her father's consigliere, and he has a firm hand in their family business. If anyone knows what it's like living with a man like Flynn, it's Gloria.

"It can be hard and knowing you, I'm guessing you will struggle with that."

"Why?"

"Because you're so independent. I remember you want to be part of your dad's business. Knowing how this world operates, I'm guessing your Flynn would assign you a bodyguard and you would never be allowed out on your own."

"Don't be ridiculous." I laugh out loud and Gloria stares at me with a serious expression. "I mean it, honey. This world is dangerous. It's why we live under close protection. There are many enemies out there who will use you against him. You will become a target and he will do everything possible to keep you alive."

I'm not liking this conversation and it must show on my face because she says gently, "Trust me, you need all the facts. I don't know Flynn, but I understand the world he operates in. It's hard, cruel, and violent, and it takes a special person to survive it."

"You don't think I can?"

I inject some steel into my voice, and she laughs out loud. "Of course, you can, but it won't come without sacrifice. Take me, for instance."

She looks across at her daughter and shakes her head sadly. "Sophia will never enjoy freedom. Her friends have been chosen based on their parentage and she will never be free to choose her own. Her life will be spent in a gilded cage, much like mine, and we sacrifice normal life for riches gained from misery. I'm not sure this will sit well with you, so consider it carefully before lust renders you blind."

I know she is right, and I shake my head and sigh. "It's not been that easy for me either, Gloria. Yes, I have my freedom, which I value above everything. But I have never really enjoyed that, anyway. I'm the daughter of a billionaire and have my own restrictions because of it. I'm included in other people's lives because of who my father is, and I'm judged because of it. Any guys that head my way are doing so because of him. Since meeting Flynn, I finally understand what it's like to be desired. He can't fake that; I see it in his eyes. He's as lost as I am, and we recognize that in one another. Maybe we won't last the distance, but any distance at all is better than never experiencing what I feel when I'm with him."

Gloria smiles softly and I see tears in her eyes. "I'm happy for you, Louisa. Really happy for you because love does have a habit of sweeping away any problems and making everything work."

As Sophia screams with laughter, I notice for the first time a small bump in Gloria's belly and shriek, "Oh my God, when?"

She looks down and laughs. "Six months. We already found out it's a boy." She rolls her eyes. "God help us."

Thinking about Rodriguez, her husband, I must agree with her there. Dark, brooding, and dangerous, he could make the sun freeze and I'm hoping she sees a softer side to him because that man scares me to death.

We spend the next hour chatting about life, and I love every minute of it. Any time spent with my uncle and his daughters is a pleasure and now I have Flynn, I really do believe my life is complete.

CHAPTER 30

FLYNN

Two days later, we are back in LA and head straight to Dimitri's apartment in the city. Wesley's texts have become more abusive and now is the perfect time to head home.

As soon as we walk inside the penthouse, there is only one thing I want and as the door closes behind us, I growl, "If your clothes aren't on that floor inside of a minute, I will ruin them forever."

I start wrenching off my own and Louisa giggles as she follows my lead.

As soon as we are naked, I sweep her into my arms and almost run to the bedroom, kicking open the door and throwing her onto the bed.

She scoots back and stares at me with so much lust in her eyes, I don't think I will last long and despite wanting to savor the moment, I just can't and growl, "This is going to be quick, but I'll make it up to you."

Just watching her chest heave and her cheeks blush causes me to groan out loud and, dropping my head between her thighs, I swipe my tongue up her center, causing her to gasp loudly. Her legs shake as the wet heat beckons me inside and as I settle between her thighs, I growl, "I'm sorry baby, I can't wait."

Just experiencing her slick walls clench my cock almost makes me cum and I don't know how I control the urge but groan as my cock enters paradise. Her low moan of passion hits me square in the heart and it feels so good to be inside my woman again. The past few days have been pure agony, and I know I can't go through that again and if I don't fuck Louisa every night for the rest of my life, I will consider it a life wasted.

As I thrust harder and faster, her legs wrap around my waist and my balls slap against the wet trail seeping from her drenched pussy. Her sweat runs to meet mine and I grab her ass and pull her in deeper, loving her cries of passion that were caused by me and lifting one leg, I drive even deeper and love how we mate like wild animals on silken sheets.

It's a glorious coupling of depravity because the things I want to do to this woman is all I can think of right now.

I can tell she is close and so am I, but out of nowhere, the need to prolong this pleasure stops me from spilling into her.

As I pull out roughly, I roll her onto her front and love how good my cock feels rubbing down the crease of her ass. She gasps as I slap her hard on those plump cheeks and then groans when I dip my fingers to flick her wet clit.

Then I hold her down with one hand while I drive my cock in from behind and she arches up and pushes back onto it, causing me to roar. While fisting her hair, I wrench her head back and drive in harder and deeper, tugging on her glorious tresses as if I'm riding a pony. She screams as the orgasm hits her hard and as my own joins in, I pump hard and fast, squeezing every last drop of cum from my cock as I fuck her raw.

As I roll to the side, she gasps, "Fuck me, that was epic."

Laughing, I pull her down to my chest and stroke her back in the first gentle act since we arrived back.

"I'm sorry, baby. I've wanted to do that since the moment we left. It's been pure torture playing the respectful boyfriend when all I wanted was to tie you to my bed and fuck you on repeat."

"Tie me to the bed." She sounds shocked, but I hear a trace of desire in her voice, and I growl, "There are a lot of things I want to do to you and not all of them are strictly honorable."

Remembering how wet she got when I slapped her ass tells me she won't be averse to a rougher kind of love and the need in her voice makes me smile as she whispers, "I'll look forward to it."

Rolling her onto her back, I grip her wrists and raise them above her head and stare deep into her eyes with a promise.

"My love is fierce, rough, and deep. I will worship your body one minute and then plunder it the next. I will be rough and gentle, and I will show you things no decent girl would ever imagine. I want the whole of you, Louisa, and will give you the whole of me in return. There is nothing I won't do for you and to you, and you have my word on that."

The passion in her eyes tells me she's happy about that and as I kiss her long, leisurely, and deeply, I am the happiest I have ever been in my life.

I WAS true to my word and by the time I shower and dress, I have fucked Louisa in every position and in every room and it's doubtful if she can even walk straight. I love seeing the happiness in her eyes and the slight flush to her cheeks. The secret smile she gives me when I catch her attention and the soft way she touches me as our hands brush together. I love everything about this woman and especially the part where she's mine. It's still hard to believe that something good has come out of something so terrible it's hard to talk about, but where we're heading next may put that particular ghost to rest.

Louisa is exhausted and I'm not surprised. She kept up with my demands but needs to sleep now. The light is fading, and she could use the rest, so I kiss her long and slowly as she lies wrapped in the silken sheets and says in a hoarse whisper, "Sleep now and restore your energy for when I return."

"Do you have to go?" She looks anxious and I groan against her lips. "I need to check in with Wesley. Hopefully, he will make this easy for me, and as soon as I have what I need, you can make the call."

Her eyes widen and I can tell she is nervous about our plan, but I need Louisa to see it through.

I whisper as I stroke her hair, "I won't let anything happen to you. Your uncle won't let anything happen to you and your father will kill us all if anything happens to you."

She nods and I hate seeing the tears glistening in her eyes and I sigh. "This is my life, baby. It's not much of one, but it's all I know. I work in the shadows. It's where I'm most at home and what I'm about to do is nothing I haven't done countless times before. If you're with me, you accept that part of me because I'm too far down this road to turn and head back."

She bites her lip and looks so troubled I want to smash something. Instead, I stroke her like a puppy dog and whisper, "Sleep, and I'll be back when you wake."

As I tear myself away from her, I'm just grateful nobody knows about us yet. Knowing she is safe makes me relax a lot and as I leave the hotel and hail a cab, I set my mind to business. Mafia business and that spells trouble for my fucking biological father.

* * *

It's strange to be back. Just heading through the gates into the fortress I call home makes me shiver with revulsion. I can understand why Angelo remodeled his entire house when his father died. Ghosts of the past aren't welcome in our future and I resolve to do exactly that when I rid the world of the scum that goes by the name of Wesley Vasquez.

Silvio stops me as I head inside and smiles with relief. "Good to see you, Flynn, he's been unbearable since you left."

"Where is he?" I'm mildly curious and the disgusted expression on Silvio's face tells me he's indulging in his usual hobby again.

"Upstairs." He raises his eyes. "He dragged some poor unfortunate girl off the streets and is making her life hell."

As a gut-wrenching scream echoes down the staircase, I roll my eyes to the heavens. "He's getting careless. He doesn't normally bring them home."

"She's the second one this week. The first one is currently taking an acid bath in the basement."

"I've had enough of this shit." I growl ominously. "Are you with me?"

Silvio looks startled. "What do you have in mind?"

"To remove him from our lives forever."

"But Massimo." The fear in his eyes reminds me why Wesley has lasted so long. Every single one of his soldiers is living under the cloud of Massimo's recriminations if anything ever happens to Wesley. It's common knowledge that he would start a blood bath and murder every one of Wesley's men if they ever turned against him, and yet the disgust in Silvio's eyes tells me I can trust him.

"I wouldn't worry about Massimo; I'm going to get him to do it for us."

"How?" The hope in Silvio's eyes makes me smile. "Watch and learn, my friend, and at the end of it, things will change for the better around here."

Silvio nods and I brief him on what he must do and as I leave him to carry out my orders, I take the stairs two at a time with a firm grip on my hunting knife.

As I near my uncle's bedroom, it sickens me to think of what's happening inside and as I grab what I need from my own room, I steal like an avenging angel down the hallway and pray this goes according to plan.

Luckily, the bastard is making so much noise he doesn't hear the door open, and he can't even see it from his position facing the wall. I can just about make out in the moonlit room his naked body pounding into a woman who is tied to the bed and looks in a bad way. Even from here, I see the blood covering her body courtesy of the knife he likes to cut them with. As sadists go, Wesley is one who knows no boundaries and often cuts and chokes his victims to death, while brutally raping every part of them he can, sometimes for days.

They are both unaware of my presence and I have practiced hard for this moment. As I edge toward the bed, I count down in my mind and as he groans, and she utters a piercing scream, I seize my chance and slam the hessian sack over the bastard's head, quickly tying it at the neck exactly as Vivian described he did to her. Karma is a bitch, and I will enjoy every minute of this.

The woman looks up in horror as Wesley bellows with rage and I place my finger on her lips and wink, causing her to stare up at me in hope. I grab my gun and knock Wesley across the side of the head, relishing his struggling body going limp in my hands. Then I tie his hands and feet together, looking in disgust at the flaccid body of a man who let it go years ago.

Gently, I untie the girl and whisper, "You're safe, darlin'. Trust me, I've got you."

She nods, the tears streaming down her face as she sobs in my arms.

Gently, I lift her off the bed and carry her from the room and call out to Silvio, who rushes immediately to my side.

"Take good care of her. Clean her up, give her money. A lot of money and make sure she has somewhere to go."

"And the boss?"

Silvio looks worried about that, and I say angrily, "You leave Wesley to me."

Turning back to the room, I can't wait to see him try to talk his way out of this one and as I retrieve my phone, I type out a text to Louisa, who may not get it until morning.

Then I drag my uncle's body behind me down the stairs to the cellar where he likes to bring his enemies to torture and take great delight in stringing him up against his own wall and leaving him to hang naked and out cold.

Slamming the door on him, I turn the key and hope the rest of the plan goes so smoothly. If it does, this will be a joy to watch.

CHAPTER 31

LOUISA

I wake aching, sore and exhausted, yet so happy I could sing like Julie Andrews. How did I get so lucky?

As I turn, I see the empty space beside me, which makes me sit up with a moment of fear. He didn't come back. My first thought is that he's ok and as I seize my phone, I see the text that tells me we're now ready for phase two of our operation and my heart starts thumping as my own part in this is up.

My fingers shake as I dial the number I hoped never to use and as the phone rings, I'm not sure my voice is up to the job.

Then a gravelly voice answers with a curious, "Massimo Delauren. Who is this?"

"Um…" My voice shakes and I dig my nails into my palm for courage. "It's um, Louisa Sullivan, your, um, niece."

"Louisa." He sounds shocked and I'm guessing he is because I've never called, or even met him once in my life and he says quickly, "Is it your father? Has something happened?"

"No, um, well, he doesn't know I'm calling you."

"I see." I sense his curiosity and his voice changes a little as he prepares for me to speak and I say hesitantly, "I hoped we could meet. I, um, well, I have some news you may want to hear."

"Then tell me; I don't like surprises." His voice is hard, and distrusting, and I whisper, "It concerns Iris Young and what she told me."

"Iris! What did she say?"

I falter and whisper, "I can't tell you over the phone. It's not safe."

"Does your father know about this?" He sounds merely curious, and I say quickly, "No, which is why we need to meet."

"No." His voice is curt. "I don't meet anyone."

"Please, uncle." I hate hearing that word on my lips, but I need to do this. "It's well, it's something you will want to discover."

There's a slight pause and then he says curtly, "I will arrange a dinner reservation. I'll bring my wife. Will you be attending alone?"

"No, I'll be accompanied by my, um, well, I believe you know him."

I wasn't expecting the low laugh that sounds down the phone and he says "Now we're getting somewhere. Who is the lucky man?"

"Flynn Vasquez."

A sharp intake of breath tells me he wasn't expecting that, and he says quickly, "You had better start explaining, young lady, if you stand any hope of my attention."

"I wouldn't call you if it wasn't in your best interests. I am putting a lot on the line for this, my own relationship with my father for one. If he learned I was going behind his back to tell you something so destructive, he would haul my ass back to Seattle and lock me up and throw away the key." My words come out in a sudden rush. "It's just that, well, Flynn came to me with a story you will very much want to hear and I'm not sure my father would approve of the company I'm keeping."

I hope he falls for it because I'm relying on his hatred of my father to hold this against him and then he laughs and whispers, "It appears you are more like me than he may be comfortable with. You have your meeting, but if I sense a trap, you won't make it out of there alive. Trust me on that."

He cuts the call, leaving me shaking as I grip the phone hard. Flynn told me he would only agree if he believed he was getting one over on my father and he wasn't wrong. The fact we used Flynn's name was the carrot on the end of the stick because he will now know Wesley has done something that Iris Young found out about.

A sudden text lights up my phone.

7.30 The Capital Room

I forward it to Flynn and lean back in my bed and try hard to calm my freaking heart down. If I make it through dinner, I'll be lucky because I'm about to have a heart attack. I'm so afraid. Even over the phone, his tone was chilling, and I hope that Flynn knows what he's doing because tonight could be both the beginning and the end for both of us.

Flynn's text does nothing to calm my beating heart, telling me he will call for me at six thirty and to stay strong until then. I'm fearful about what's happening with his uncle and try to distract myself by working on my laptop. Brad is pissed I took time off, but my father made my excuses personally, so it's doubtful he would ever complain about it and once again, I wonder what my father was on when he tried to set me up with such a dick.

I work hard for most of the day, grateful to have something to occupy my mind and as six thirty rolls ever closer, I take great care in my appearance and mentally prepare myself for what could prove to be a life changing evening.

"Honey, I'm home."

The one voice I longed for all day calls from the door, and I run at speed toward him and fall into his arms.

"It's ok, baby. Nothing happened."

I check him over anxiously and notice how tired he looks, but there's something different about him.

"What happened?"

"Wesley is where we need him, despite waking up and hollering like a psychotic demon. I've spent the day enjoying briefing my soldiers on their new life if all goes according to plan.

"What do you mean?" He takes my hand and leads me to the couch and pulls me against him, sighing with pleasure. "If Massimo does what I'm guessing he will, Wesley will be out of my life for good. That means I step up and become the Don in his place."

"The Don?" My eyes are wide as I finally realize just what I signed up for, and Flynn nods wearily. "It's good though. The men are on my side, and we can finally change things for the better. As well as my friends and your father, along with your uncle's help, we will have the resources to challenge Massimo when he makes his move. I'm not pretending this will be easy, but it's set the wheels in motion of a plan that's been years in the making."

He looks so tired I'm concerned for him because he must have had no sleep at all. The fact he has showered and now wears a black suit paired with a black silk shirt, tells me he's returned home, and I hope I haven't lost him to the madness he surrounds himself with.

In fact, seeing Flynn as he is now, mafia born and bred, it fills me with a sense of unease because how can I measure up to be the woman he needs in his life? It's obvious how powerful he is, just the aura surrounding him tells me he's stepped up and accepted a situation he was raised for.

He turns and looks at me and says huskily, "If this meeting wasn't so important, I would fuck you with that blue silk dress around your waist, spread out on that window for the whole city to watch."

"You're a wicked man, Flynn Vasquez." I can't help laughing and he shifts, pulling me onto his lap, causing my dress to ride high up my thighs. Running his hand along them, he growls, "When this hellish night is over, I'm spending the rest of it inside you, and that's a promise."

Tilting my face to his, he whispers, "You look beautiful, baby. That color really complements your eyes."

He brushes his lips against mine and whispers, "So fuckable and all mine. How did I get so lucky?"

The tears glisten like diamonds in my eyes because I'm the lucky one. I never for one moment thought I'd meet a man like him who made me feel so desired and special. Flynn Vasquez is an Angel sent from God and he has stolen my heart.

CHAPTER 32

FLYNN

I don't get nervous ever, but tonight is the exception to that rule. So much is riding on this, and it has to be a success, otherwise I will have failed my mission. There is still no word on the whereabouts of Massimo's daughter even though Malik has been searching, using every resource he has. I just hope we get to her before Massimo does otherwise, we will have lost a vital weapon in our Arsenal.

The Capital Room is always Massimo's preferred choice and every seat in the place will be filled with his men. Massimo likes to conduct his business there but under the close guard of his trusted soldiers.

As we enter the restaurant, I can tell that Louisa is nervous and I grip her hand hard, desperate to reassure her. Dimitri has equipped us with state-of-the-art listening devices and Pedro is standing by with his men to get us out of trouble if it starts going to shit.

The thing I'm most nervous about, though, is seeing Winter for the first time since college. I not sure how I'm going to control myself around her and physically ache for one hungry glance at her. Winter is the catalyst driving this, but even without her, we would be treading this path. It's just more urgent now.

The waiter shows us to the middle table, and I note the curious glances of the other diners. Massimo's men and their wives or girlfriends. I'm in no doubt about that and as we move through them, I sense their eyes burning a hole in my back. Louisa seems on edge, and I squeeze her hand reassuringly as we take our seats and stare at the menu.

We don't speak out of fear of being overheard, and my thumping heart counts down to the bastard's arrival.

Exactly on the dot of seven thirty, they arrive, and the air stills as pure evil enters the room. I stand out of respect and Louisa looks with interest at the woman beside a man old enough to be her father.

Nothing prepares me for the automaton that glides into the room beside her husband. It's as if her soul is under lock and key because there is zero recognition or emotion in those dark eyes shrouded in mystery.

My first view of Winter in what is well over a year is not a good one. Gone is the happy, warm person she was and in its place is the cool, emotionless shell of the vivacious soul that once lived there. Her long black hair gleams as if waxed and hangs long down her back. She is wearing a red silk dress that outlines her slender frame and her perfectly made-up face accentuates a cold, hard beauty. She doesn't even glance in our direction and glides rather than walks beside her aging husband.

Massimo himself rests a possessive arm on hers and I want to tear him apart with my bare hands for even touching the woman I have sworn to set free. Could I take him out now? I already know the answer to that which doesn't make this situation any better. I wonder how Angelo held it together when he was in the same position as I am now and if anything, it hardens my resolve to end her nightmare and send her captor to hell, where he will fit in nicely.

I nod with respect as Massimo stares at me as if he wants to kill me outright, and I suppose he does. For all he knows, I am his son; the one who caused the death of the only woman he ever loved.

There are no pleasantries as Massimo says darkly, "Take a seat."

He holds out Winter's chair and I steal a look at possibly the kindest woman I have ever met and the most tragic. She barely reacts. It's as if she is frozen and has no life left in her and my heart twists in agony at the suffering she must live through every day.

"Louisa, my darling niece." Massimo has obviously decided she is the safer option here, and I sense her shiver with revulsion as he turns his attention to her.

"You are the image of your mother, such a terrible tragedy. You have my condolences, my dear."

"Thank you." Louisa can barely get the words out and as the waiter fills our glasses, the conversation stalls and is replaced by menace.

He moves away and Massimo says gruffly, "What's the big secret you couldn't wait to tell me?"

He directs his question to Louisa, but I'm guessing he is anticipating being told that I know he is my father. It's almost amusing to string this out and then lay the killer blow, but I can't stop staring at Winter, who gazes down at her plate as if she needs winding up.

"Well…"

Louisa takes a deep breath. "Flynn came to visit us in Seattle because of something he was told. He was after answers and it's best if he tells the story."

She leans back and I raise my guard and say in a dull voice,

"My father's consigliere was shot and with his last breath, he told me to find two people. Iris Young and Vivian Clark."

Massimo nods but obviously doesn't remember my mother and I say in a voice devoid of emotion. "I discovered Vivian was married to your brother, Dimitri, and flew to Seattle to discover the truth." I fix him a dark stare which only makes him smile with a sick, twisted look of satisfaction on his face.

"She told me she had been raped and beaten and left for dead."

I glance at Winter for any reaction, but she continues staring at her plate.

Massimo shrugs. "Why does that concern me?"

"Because Wesley Vasquez told her it was you."

I fix him with a searching look and to his credit, he looks shocked about that.

"He said it was me." He says it slowly, as if confirming the details in his mind, and I nod.

"She became pregnant, and I was the result of that." He still doesn't react even though he believes differently, and I say roughly, "She was told the baby had died."

There is no reaction from Winter, and I wonder if she's even listening, and Massimo shrugs. "I still don't understand what that has to do with me. Wesley was mistaken. Your visit is a futile one."

He looks bored already and so I dive straight in. "So, I turned to the next name on the list for answers and searched for Iris Young."

Massimo looks up with interest. "And did you find her?"

I watch a steely glint flash in his eyes as I nod. "I visited her with Louisa, and she told us a very interesting story."

Massimo looks angry and I'm guessing he hates knowing we were granted access to her, and I wouldn't want to be in the manager's shoes when he goes looking for answers.

"What did she say?"

Again, Massimo merely looks interested, and I say roughly, "I introduced myself as your son and she denied it. She told me you never had a son."

"She's old and riddled with dementia. She was wrong."

Massimo sighs heavily. "The truth is, Flynn, Wesley told your mother a lie. She isn't your mother, but I am your father, as it happens."

He grins, hoping I will be shocked, emotional even, so he can disown me all over again. Perhaps rant at me for killing his beloved wife, so I lean back in my chair and shake my head. "Actually, you're wrong. She told me you had a baby, but it was a girl."

For the first time, the blood drains from Massimo's face and he appears speechless. So, I carry on relentlessly aiming blow upon well prepared blow.

"She told me the baby was born shortly before Imogen hemorrhaged and died. The doctor arrived too late to save her, and she called Wesley because you were out of town at the time. They agreed you were never to discover you had a girl. You would blame her for the death of your wife and the fact you wanted a son would guarantee her suffering."

"Wesley said that?" I watch the anger flare in Massimo's eyes as he curls his fist and Louisa interrupts. "Wesley told Iris that he heard about an abandoned baby. The mother didn't want him, and they agreed on a swap. Flynn was that baby and apparently Wesley used him to protect himself by making you believe he was taking on your hated child, promising to make his life a living hell for causing the death of your wife, guaranteeing his own safety in the process. You would be indebted to him, and he would live under your protection. We now believe that Wesley was Flynn's father and the man who raped Vivian Clark."

We watch in fascination as Massimo's rage spills out and his crazed expression should scare me right now, but all I can think of is delivering the final blow.

"So, I've come to you with a deal."

Massimo looks up sharply. "Which is?"

"I deliver you Wesley to deal with as you wish, and I take over as the head of his family."

Massimo leans forward and says darkly, "Does Wesley know this?"

"Wesley knows nothing." I twist my mouth into an evil grin and growl, "I interrupted him raping another woman and he is currently shackled to the wall of his own torture chamber. I decided to offer him to you as a sign of my loyalty."

"Your loyalty." I glance casually at Winter and if anything, she looks even more stiff than before, and I swear I see her lower lip tremble before it freezes back into place.

"You want to replace Wesley as my trusted friend?"

Massimo laughs darkly. "An interesting situation. The man I thought was my hated son turns out to be an imposter who is offering up his own father to me as a sacrifice." He shakes his head and laughs darkly. "I love it. It's perfect. I almost wish you were my son."

Then he slips the mask back in place and says roughly, "Why should I believe you?"

"You don't have to believe me. You can hear it for yourself."

Without another word, I pick up my phone and press play and the entire conversation we had with Iris Young plays out in glorious stereo. With every word, Massimo gets even angrier and as the conversation ends, he thumps his fist loudly on the table, causing the glasses to crash to the floor.

Still, Winter looks down and as he lifts the bottle of wine and hurls it through the window, we all stare in shock at the red liquid spilling against the clear glass like blood from a massacred body.

Massimo appears unhinged as he thumps the table in a

steady beat and mutters under his breath. His men appear nervous around us, and the atmosphere is so tense anything could happen.

A slight movement opposite diverts my attention, and I watch in fascination as Winter raises her hand and rests it calmly on Massimo's arm. Just that one gesture confuses me. She *is* in there, but why offer him comfort? What the fuck is going on and why won't she look at me?

It appears to do the trick as Massimo gets his breathing under control and looks at his wife with an expression that almost makes me believe he loves her. "I'm sorry, my darling, you are right to check me."

He lifts her hand and kisses it in a public show of affection, and I'm horrified when she looks at him and smiles lovingly.

"I love you darling."

She smiles sweetly and just hearing her soft voice again drives a knife through my heart. Massimo visibly relaxes and twists her long black hair in his fingers and sighs with pleasure.

"I am such a lucky man. My wife is an angel sent to me from God. She is the only one who can calm my temper and…" He breaks off. "Oh, I forgot that you two have already met."

I don't miss the cunning gleam in his eyes he says to her, "Isn't Flynn one of your brother's friends, darling? I'm certain you all shared a house at Rockwell Academy. Well, this is nice? Two friends meeting up at last."

As I stare in shock, Winter turns her attention to me, and I'm not even sure she is looking at me at all as she says in a stilted voice. "Flynn was my brother's friend. We rarely spoke."

For some reason, I can tell it's important that I back her up and I nod. "It's true. I kept my distance because Angelo told us to. Winter lived with her friend Emma at the top of the house, and we never mixed."

Massimo's eyes flash as he stares between us and then

snarls, "That aside. Where is your... well, where is Wesley now?"

"I told you, chained up and awaiting his fate. Either by your hand or mine."

Massimo looks at me with approval for the first time and nods. Then he looks across at Louisa and smiles. "You did well, my dear, bringing this to my attention and have no fear, I won't be telling your father of your visit. In fact, I doubt I'll ever speak to him again." He sighs heavily. "It's such a shame when families are torn apart, isn't that right, Winter?"

If he is looking for a reaction, he doesn't get one as she merely nods, saying in her perfectly controlled voice. "Such a shame."

Massimo sighs loudly. "My own wife can't bear to be around her brother. I have tried so many times to bring them together, but she is so reliant on me she can't bear to be away from me for a second. Isn't that right, my darling?"

"Yes, my darling." Winter looks at Massimo as if he is her one true love and I feel sick to my stomach. Something isn't right and then Massimo says in a voice laced with pure evil.

"I will take delivery of Wesley later tonight. I thank you for bringing this matter to my attention and before we bring this to a conclusion, I would like to know just one thing."

"Of course." I already know what's coming, and I was right, as he says with a slight break to his voice.

"Have you discovered my daughter's whereabouts?"

I almost laugh out loud because as if I would tell him if I did.

Instead, I shake my head and pretend to be upset.

"I'm sorry, I don't. Perhaps Iris Young will be more forthcoming to you. I'm afraid our conversation was interrupted before she could reveal where she went."

Massimo nods and I'm guessing Iris is about to get a visit outside of normal hours and I'm not surprised when he stands and helps Winter to her feet before saying, "Please forgive my rudeness, but we have much to arrange. I would be honored if you enjoyed your meal at my expense and I will enjoy many years of loyal service from you, Flynn. You did the right thing in bringing this to my attention and Louisa..." He turns and fixes her with a soft smile. "You can always come to me if you need anything. I am your humble servant."

Louisa says gruffly, "Thank you, um, uncle."

As they head from the room, I'm not surprised when the other diners stand and follow them, revealing I was right about their identity. As we sit alone in the emptied restaurant, Louisa breathes a huge sigh of relief.

"What the fuck? I've never been so scared in my life, and someone has got to help that poor woman. There's something seriously wrong there."

I nod, my heart twisting in pain as I witnessed first-hand Winter's suffering. I'm not sure if we can wait for the plan to work out because something is telling me she doesn't have long.

CHAPTER 33

LOUISA

As soon as we leave the restaurant, Flynn says with a hint of impatience in his voice. I'm so sorry. We must return home to deal with Wesley. I should arrange his transportation.

He turns to me and says gently, "Perhaps you should head back to the hotel. I'll take you and then return when I've dealt with Wesley."

"No."

Flynn looks surprised and I say firmly, "I want to know the whole of you, Flynn, even if that scares me to death. I want to meet your uncle and I want to see where you were brought up. I don't care if it's dangerous, shocking, or despicable. I desire the whole of you, Flynn, all the jagged edges and sharp corners. I want to learn the cruelty of your life and understand how you were formed."

"No, Louisa." Flynn appears angry and I grab his face in my hands and press my lips against his to silence him. Pulling away I whisper, "Let me in, Flynn. You're not on your own anymore, and I need to do this. You *need* me to do this, and if we are to stand any chance of surviving this life, we must stick together."

I'm surprised when he pulls me roughly against him and kisses me so deeply it takes my breath away and then he growls, "Be careful what you wish for, baby. You are about to head on a one-way ticket to hell."

* * *

I can tell Flynn is on edge. The closer we get to his home, the quieter he gets and as we pass through huge electric gates, I look out on a landscape that screams intimidation. Even though I'm used to living in a large house with all the trappings of wealth, this is like venturing into Hogwarts. It's gloomy, threatening and frightening. It's probably where Stephen King comes for inspiration for his horror stories, and I am already regretting my impulsive decision to come here.

Flynn has obviously been seized by the circling demons because there's an aura of despair in the car that intensifies the closer we get to the house of horrors. Clearing my throat, I try to think of something complimentary to say, nice even but can only come up with, "It's, well, um…"

"Hell, baby. Welcome to hell."

Flynn cuts me off and brings his Ferrari to a screeching halt outside a huge oak door and he exhales sharply. "Like I said, be careful what you wish for because you may want to change yours."

He turns and I see an expression of resignation on his face as he sighs. "You, though, can always change your mind. Say the word and I'll turn around and take you back to the apartment."

"No." I try to stop my voice from trembling. "I want to understand you, and I'm guessing this is going to tell me everything I need to know."

"You may decide it's too much. A lot to take on and regret

your decision. What happens if you change your mind about me—us?"

For the first time since I met him, Flynn seems a little unsure. He's always been so strong, self-assured, and confident. I suppose I'm so used to being that person myself I understand far more what he's going through and so I grip his hand firmly and tug him sharply against me, saying fiercely, "Nothing will ever change how I feel about you. How could it when you are kind, loving, and considerate?"

He rests his head against mine and says with a sigh, "I'll ask you that question again when we leave. Prepare for a crash course in misery, baby, because the next few hours will never leave you and I will say it again. Just tell me and I'll turn this car around and save you from possibly the worst experience of your life."

"And I'll say it again. No!"

With a deep sigh, he nods toward the house. "Then let me show you what pain looks like. Humiliation, hatred, and revulsion. Open your eyes and see what happens when your sins catch up with you and what a monster fear molds even the most reluctant man into."

He turns away and leaves the car, rounding it to open my door and as he takes my hand, he grips it hard and whispers, "I will never let anything happen to you. This is the reality of my life, and you will understand why I have been driven to this point."

I fall silent as we head inside and are transported into what appears to be like an ancient castle. Dark wood paneling creates a somber welcome, and I half expect flaming torches on the wall, instead of the huge ornate chandeliers and wall sconces that are lit with a warm glow. There are no modern touches, just dusty looking antiques and ancient looking paintings residing behind gold, heavy frames. It's a little overwhelming because there are no women's touches anywhere and the whole vibe is one of intimidation and secrecy.

A man appears, who nods to me and fixes Flynn with an anxious look. "He's getting more irate by the second. I hoped he would have calmed down by now, but he has the resilience of a devil."

"Let him shout all he likes. His ride out of here leaves in less than an hour."

"What do you mean?" The guy looks a little wary of me and Flynn pulls me forward. "This is Louisa, my girlfriend. She knows everything, so you can relax."

Being described as Flynn's girlfriend causes a warm fluffy emotion to spread through me, casting light on shade. It's so good to be with him and despite all of this, I wouldn't want to be anywhere else but his side and to my surprise, the man's face breaks out into a smile, and he nods with approval, making me feel a lot better about myself.

"Silvio, ma'am. Welcome to damnation."

He winks and shares an amused glance with Flynn, who rolls his eyes and grips my hand a little tighter. "Well, Louisa has requested that I show her my home and the first stop should be meeting the family, don't you agree?"

Silvio looks wary of that. "Are you sure? I mean…"

"I'm sure." My own voice rings out, determined and defiant, and Silvio laughs softly. "Then welcome, ma'am, and you have my assurance that everybody here, with one exception maybe, will protect you with their life."

My eyes widen as I sense the power Flynn now has because he has an army of men behind him who are intent on keeping him alive. I know how it works. Uncle Pedro has the exact same loyalty and now seeing it first-hand, it reminds me what I've signed up for.

Gloria was right. My life is about to change and just thinking of living in this place gives me the creeps. Almost as if he can read my mind, Flynn says out loud, "When Louisa moves in, prepare for demolition. This place will be knocked down and rebuilt and there will be nothing left of the old ways."

Silvio grins. "I'm happy about that."

Flynn turns and stares at me long and hard, as if he's deep in thought, which is a little unnerving, really. It's almost as if he's preparing himself for something and then he says in a deep, husky voice, "Are you ready to meet Satan himself?"

To be honest, I'm not, but part of me is curious about the man who has made Flynn's life a living hell and so I nod. "As I'll ever be."

Silvio shakes his head and turns and as we follow him, I offer up a prayer to keep us safe and deliver us from this madness.

CHAPTER 34

FLYNN

It feels strange escorting Louisa to the basement, where I have chained my naked uncle to the wall. I'm pretty certain she won't enjoy the experience half as much as I will. If anything concerns me, it's that she will never look at me in the same way again. Women don't get to see the harsh reality of our life. They are protected and cherished and live in a bubble protecting them from the evil world we live in. But Louisa is different, and I love her for that. So strong, curious, probably foolish but independent and knows her own mind and I would never treat her any less than my equal. However, now that I've found her, I'm desperate to keep her and this will be the biggest test of our relationship so far.

As Silvio turns the key and slides back the huge iron bolt, I'm more anxious about what Louisa thinks than anything else.

As we enter the room, she grips my hand a little tighter and an eerie silence wraps around us, making me wonder if my uncle has passed out. Then a low laugh of pure evil reaches out and claws at my senses, and his voice slides across my soul like the slithering snake he is.

"So, you showed up at last. Maybe now we can make some progress."

I say nothing and grip Louisa's hand a little tighter as he casts his devilish eyes over her and laughs out loud. "Is that the best you could do? I knew you were mad but come on, Flynn, where's your taste?"

Dropping Louisa's hand, I step forward and punch him hard around the head, causing her to gasp and the blood to coat my knuckles. To my uncle's credit, he merely laughs as I growl, "Louisa is the most beautiful woman on the planet and don't you dare even look at her, you dirty bastard."

My uncle spits blood and growls, "You've made your point. Now cut me down and tell me what this is all about. We both know you won't get away with this, so make it easy on yourself and your punishment will be a little less severe."

I stare at Silvio in astonishment because my uncle really believes he's still calling the shots around here and that this is just a weak show of power to make a point.

Stepping back, I pull out my phone and say darkly, "The reason you are hanging from your own torture chamber is because of a conversation I had with a woman you once knew."

As I press play, Iris's voice sounds loud in the confined space and, as she speaks, Wesley looks up in surprise. As the words hit home, I see the expression in his eyes change in a heartbeat and Silvio's gasp of surprise tells me even he knows how serious this is.

Betrayal is a terrible thing when you are caught and the fact the man you went against is the biggest monster in the pack makes it all the worse and as Iris Young spills Wesley's darkest secret, he starts shivering and not just from the cold.

"I'll set you free, I'll give you money, anything, just delete that recording."

It's interesting that he thinks he has a choice here and I laugh into the gloom, with all the madness of my past spilling into the atmosphere. "Even now, you are trying to save your own skin. You will do anything to protect yourself; you always have. As long as you're ok, nothing or no one else matters."

I spit on his face and growl, "You hide behind your men and only venture out when the coast is clear. You pick on those more defenseless than you to stroke your own over-inflated ego. You rape, torture, and murder innocent women for pleasure and hide behind locked doors when your own men are under attack, only coming out when you are sure the threat has gone. You are a coward, a bully, and the most despicable man I have ever met. And the fact I am the result of that, is the reason the madness lives inside my soul. Well, not anymore, uncle, or should I call you daddy?"

Wesley shouts, "You only have the ramblings of a senile old woman to go on. She's mad, can't you see that? You're wrong, you are Massimo's son and he asked me to make your life a living hell. I have carried out my end of the bargain and he will protect me. This is your madness, Flynn, your fabrication just to get what you want, and he will gut you like a pig for my enjoyment when he learns what you have done."

"That's interesting." I step back and twist my mouth into a sadistic grin. "He didn't seem so happy when I played this recording to him less than an hour ago."

You could cut the tension with a sweep of the finger as all hope drains from Wesley's face and he loses all his fight in an instant. He starts to shake as he whispers, "Massimo knows."

"Yes uncle, he knows everything, and he didn't seem too pleased, did he Louisa?"

It makes me smile when a strong voice rings out, "No, I would even say he looked angry. I don't think I've experienced rage quite like it."

To my surprise, she moves and stands by my side and fixes him with a dark glare. "It's funny how sins have a habit of catching up with you. To be honest, I'm glad I met you, Mr.

Vasquez, because now I can put a face to the name of the monster who stars in Flynn's nightmares. And do you know what? You're not that special. In fact, I would even go as far to say you're a big disappointment because I was expecting someone strong, but all I see is a coward, a bully, and a dying man. Enjoy the transition to Hell, Mr. Vasquez. I'm guessing they are preparing a place for you as we speak."

She steps back and says roughly, "Do what you must, Flynn. Get this bastard out of your system and don't hold back. I'm happy to watch."

Silvio's low laugh makes me smile because God knows, I fall in love with Louisa all over again.

CHAPTER 35

LOUISA

I sense the rage burning through my body, searing every part of it and causing the fire to burn brightly. Meeting Wesley makes everything slot into place. The pain in his son's eyes as he struggles to deal with the cards life dealt him. The madness that he lives with every day as he carries out his uncle's wishes, never really understanding what he did to deserve such misery. The fact he's such a gentleman is the most surprising thing of all when he's had this bastard as a role model and yet picturing Vivian's kindness, I'm glad he received a lot more than her looks when she gave birth to him. Luckily for him, he swerved any of Wesley's personality and when he stares into the mirror, I'm hoping the memory of Wesley will diminish over time.

I wasn't sure what I'd find when I came here. How I'd feel walking into this house of sin. However, I'm relieved that I've found every answer I was looking for because this is a life I can deal with. It's surprised me more than anything that I am not sickened by what I see. The dark, torture chamber of the damned shocked me at first and then I was glad to be here to witness the tough retribution that only a man like Wesley deserves. I'm guessing Flynn would never bring anyone here who hadn't earned every minute of it and if this is his life, I understand the reasons why a lot better.

Gloria doesn't think I can cope with this. That I'm not strong enough—I am. In fact, I almost wish I could murder the bastard myself for Flynn because when I picture the torment this man has put him through all his life makes me madder than Satan and every bit as evil.

So, I step back, and hope Flynn makes this a long, slow, torturous death, but am surprised when he laughs out loud.

"Well, this was nice, and it's good to catch up, but I don't want to waste any more of my life on you."

"What do you mean?" Wesley almost sounds hopeful, thinking he will be freed and Flynn steps forward and says with a great deal of satisfaction. "I promised to deliver you to Massimo this evening. One thing I always do, uncle, is deliver on my promises."

Wesley's agonized scream is surprising because it appears the anticipation of it is causing him more pain than anything else and Flynn looks first at me and then at Silvio and the light in his eyes dances around the gloom like a firefly.

"This is interesting. You fear the thought of what's coming more than anything that has happened so far. I wonder if that's what the women felt when you got your disgusting hands on them. Did you listen to their screams and spare any compassion for them? My mother, for example."

Flynn steps forward and grasps his face in his hands and squeezes hard, causing Wesley's eyes to bulge and his face to turn red. He snarls, "Did you care for Logan as he lay dying on the ground as a result of all the loyal years of service? Did you care about the emotional damage you did to my mother when you told her that her baby had died before trapping him in a lifetime of hell with you? No, I'm guessing not and now those sins are catching up with you because your biggest mistake in life isn't in my creation. It's betraying the man who you called your best friend to ensure your own miserable safety. It's lying to him and taking away the one thing that could have saved him from the madness he lives with every day, and it's amusing that the insanity in him will be your own painful downfall."

Flynn steps back. "I almost wish I had the pleasure myself, but knowing he could do a much better job of it fills me with happiness.

Flynn looks at his uncle with disgust as Wesley pisses on the ground in fear and starts to shake violently, pleading, "Please son…" He doesn't get to say another word because with a roar, Flynn's fist cracks his skull and the scream that causes bounces off the walls mingling with the tortured ghosts of the past. As he slumps forward, still hanging by his wrists, Flynn turns to Silvio and sighs with relief. "Thank God I never have to hear that whining bastard's voice again. Deliver him to evil and there is no need to pray for his soul."

He looks across the dingy room and as his eyes find mine, the fierce love I see burning in them makes my breath hitch and my heart beat faster because Flynn has dealt with his past and is now facing his future and I am the lucky one who gets to see what that involves.

WE WALK hand in hand away from the madness and the disgusting remains of the man who deserves everything coming to him and as we step back into civilization, Flynn says wearily, "This may be our home now, Louisa but if I recognize one brick in it by the time you have changed it forever, I won't be happy."

"What do you mean?" The excitement starts building as he turns and pulls me close to him and stares deeply into my eyes. "It means that I want to marry you, look after you, have a family with you and love you forever because you are the family I never believed I'd find. You are the woman I never knew was out there waiting for me, and you are my motivation and reason for living."

Then he kisses me long and slowly and after a while, he pulls back and whispers, "This is our first good memory in a place filled with nothing but bad ones. We will make this house a happy one and I know I'm asking a lot, but will you walk into the madness with me, Louisa, and make me happy for once in my life?"

I don't even hesitate and say huskily, "Yes, Flynn, of course I will. I love you."

He looks shocked, as if he forgot such a word existed and I reach up and touch the palm of my hand to his face and whisper, "I love you, Flynn and I always will."

The emotion in his eyes makes the tears run freely down my face as we share a moment that changes both our lives. His own hand closes against mine and he says with a low growl, "I love you too, Louisa. I can finally say that knowing I have a chance of keeping it. Knowing I deserve it and knowing I mean it. I love your smile, your beautiful soul, and your fierce loyalty. I love the passion and fire in your eyes and your beautiful body. I love your intelligence and your kindness and most of all I love being inside you where I am happiest, so I'm done with talking and we need to get the fuck out of here, so I can show you just how much I love you all night long."

He doesn't even wait for my response and tugs me after him as if there's a fire and as we head outside to his waiting car, I can't wait for what happens next.

CHAPTER 36

FLYNN

I don't deserve Louisa. A woman like that isn't meant for a man like me. Good, honest, kind and courageous. When she stood by my side with no fear and squared up to my uncle, I fell even deeper under her spell. The fact she accepted the situation and even appeared to relish it, deepened that love and I have never seen a more beautiful woman than the one who stood by my side and now it's up to me to prove to her that I am worthy of her love.

Leaving Silvio to deal with the garbage, we head to my apartment in town because the last thing I want is to make love to Louisa in this torture chamber, so we head off and it amazes me to find that I leave the part of me that feared the future behind. The despair stays with it along with the loneliness because I have the most amazing woman by my side now and I will make our lives a happier one and will kill anyone who gets in the way of that.

My love is a fierce destructive force of nature that burns inside. I may not change who I am and what I do, but I can make it count for something. I will always be mafia; I know that and yet I will be a husband and a father first. Now it's even more important that we rid the world of scum like Massimo, so we can mold this life into one we can live with, for all our sakes.

Louisa shifts in her seat and I tell she's as excited as I am to get to our destination and I laugh softly when she says huskily, "Where are we going?"

"To my apartment. I thought you might like to see where I go to escape."

"I would."

Her soft hand grasps my own and as our fingers lock together, I'm glad it isn't far.

The soft classical music plays out from the speakers, which has always calmed the rage inside me but now she does a much better job of that and as we speed away from my past into our future, I don't even spare a thought for my uncle who is being despatched to hell right now.

As we pull into the underground car park, I'm just glad to be home and bringing a woman here is a first for me. To be with the same woman for longer than one night only is a first for me and a surprising pleasure, which I suppose I always knew it would be.

Until Louisa, I never let emotion into my life. I treated my women well for one night and then walked away. I am not my uncle. I would never hurt a woman and now I have so much love to give the right one.

We enter the elevator and I pull her into my arms and love how good she feels against me. As I stroke her hair, I hold her close and whisper, "This is so good."

"What, my hair?" She chuckles softly against my chest, and I grin. "No, being here with you. I never thought it would happen, but thank fuck it did because I wouldn't want to miss this for anything."

She leans back and drags my face down to meet hers and

says huskily, "You have made me a woman, Flynn, *your* woman, and I will never let you down."

As she kisses me hungrily, I am so done with talking and as the elevator reaches its destination, I pull her into my apartment and growl, "You can take the tour later. I can't wait another minute."

Tearing off my clothes, I watch her do the same and we don't make it past the first step into my apartment before I push her against the wall and kick her legs apart, taking a moment to appreciate the flush on her face. The lust in her eyes and the incredible beauty this woman possesses makes me quite emotional as I push in hard and fast and love her gasp of pleasure as her walls clench my cock and own it all over again.

This isn't soft, loving, or slow, this is fucking at its most desperate. As I pound into her against the wall, it's frantic and animalistic, and her loud scream of pleasure makes me even harder.

"Fuck Flynn, this is so good."

I want to drag her pleasure out slowly, inch by inch, and fill her with love because she deserves the best of everything I can give her.

I lift her away from the wall and push her roughly to the floor and as we hit the deck, I pull her on top of me so that my back is against the cold marble. I'm loving seeing her astride me as she slides down onto my throbbing cock and as I slowly fill her completely, I stare in wonder at the flushed face infused with happiness as she bites down on her lip and groans in ecstasy.

Just watching her fuck me makes me even harder and for once I lie back and observe an angel at work. She moves like an erotic image in all my dreams and the sexual dance she is giving me right now is pleasure at its spiciest. Just her grinding against my cock fills me with so much passion I want to prolong this all night and so, spinning her to one side, I lift her leg and drive even deeper, loving how she cries out as I hit the spot.

Her scream of pleasure makes me feel like a king as she shudders against me and rides the wave that's crashing through her entire body. I stare in fascination as she gives into the pleasure and she has never looked more beautiful as she comes apart on my cock. It's too much to hold back and with a roar I come so hard I am blinded for a moment, and I don't think I have ever come so hard in my life. Fucking with emotion is my new favorite hobby and I intend on practicing hard every hour I can. I don't think I'll ever get enough of this woman, and I almost pity her because now I've found her, my love will be relentless and if anyone can cope with that, I'm in no doubt she can.

THE NEXT MORNING dawns and waking up with Louisa in my arms is a miracle that will never get old. Her warm body against mine heats my soul and, as she stirs, I drop a light kiss on her neck.

"Morning angel."

Her soft sigh of pleasure makes me smile and I whisper, "I hope you slept well, because I want to fuck you all day."

Her low laugh makes me grin like the village idiot, and she says with pretend weariness, "You're a caveman."

As I slide into her before she wakes fully, her eyes snap open and her gasp makes me smile.

"Really, Flynn."

Her words don't match her expression as I gently rock inside her and as her legs wrap around my waist, I drive even deeper, loving how wet, warm, and delicious she is. I run my thumb against her nipple and relish her soft moan of pleasure and as I gently nip her neck, the rush of wet heat tells me she's loving every minute of this.

This time I make love to Louisa slowly and with care, building up to her release with a slow pleasure that is nothing like the frantic coupling when we stepped foot inside this apartment last night. Her low moans of pleasure fill my heart with light, and just like that, Louisa Sullivan is my newest plaything. I will play with her all day and night and be happy to lose myself from life for as long it takes to sate the thirst I have for her because it never seems to diminish.

As she cries out and she bites her lip, I stare in wonder as she experiences an orgasm of the most intense kind.

This is what I love, seeing the pleasure my body brings to hers and for once, my own can wait. I'm not interested in rushing this because I want to see how many times I can make her come before my own stops play.

CHAPTER 37

LOUISA

If I was under the illusion bed meant sleep, I was so wrong. I had two orgasms before Flynn dragged me from the bed and now we are sitting in his state-of-the-art kitchen as naked as nature intended, devouring the breakfast he ordered up from the local deli.

Soft pastries and light fluffy pancakes cause my diet to fail miserably, and I couldn't give a fuck. Flynn obviously gets pleasure from seeing me eat and the soft smile of approval on his lips as I groan with longing is the sweetest sight.

In fact, breakfast with Flynn is an interesting one because he surprised me by demanding I lie on his kitchen floor while he drizzled maple syrup all over my body. Then he proceeded to lick every last drop, and I will never look at pancakes in quite the same way again. In fact, even breakfast was a sexual act and as he ate his own from between my tits, my thighs and from my own mouth, I came hard again, making me doubt I'll ever be able to keep up with him.

Even when we shower, he runs his hands all over my body and as the water washes away the sticky heat; he drops to his knees and buries his face between my thighs and sucks and licks until I come apart all over again. When he pulls me from the shower and dries us both in a warm towel, I return the favor and love the way he slides to the back of my throat as I suck him hard.

As we clean our teeth, he wraps one arm around my body and eases in from behind and pushes me against the sink as he thrusts into me hard before he drags me back to bed and worships me all over again until I pass out with exhaustion.

I WAKE with the sunlight warming my body through the huge panoramic window with Flynn's limbs tangled in mine. He is sleeping soundly, and I watch him for a moment, loving the peaceful expression on the most beautiful face I have ever seen. I still can't accept he's mine and wants me as much as I do him and now I am a firm believer in miracles because God had delivered every prayer I ever offered him and even the fact he's mafia doesn't matter.

When I saw his uncle chained to the wall, the thing that shocked me the most was the excitement I felt. It was a rush watching an evil man get what he deserves, and I wonder what that says about me. Perhaps I'm darker in spirit that even I thought and knowing this man flush against me is capable of so many dark deeds, makes me wild with passion. Possibly I'm the monster here, not him, because I'm kind of loving the dark side of him even more than the light.

"What are you thinking?" His voice startles me and I glance up and note his soft smile of amusement as he stares deep into my eyes.

"Not much, just about how much I enjoyed seeing you work yesterday."

The surprise in his eyes makes me laugh out loud, and he shakes his head in wonder. "I knew you were the woman for me, Louisa Sullivan. Underneath that angelic façade is a wicked woman clawing to get out."

"You better believe it."

He laughs and then groans as his phone vibrates angrily on the bedside table.

"I should get this." He pulls away with a reluctant sigh and slips from the bed, phone in hand.

As he stands by the window and looks down on the city below, I admire his naked body like a lust crazy harlot salivating over anything he can give me.

"Malik."

I watch the excitement building and I wonder what he's hearing right now. Obviously, whatever it is makes his eyes gleam with pleasure that tells me it's good news at least, and he growls, "I'll be right there."

As he cuts the call, he takes a moment to gaze out on the city and when he turns, I see what I've signed up. The Mafia Don is back in the room and the power that flashes from his eyes makes me wet and ready to go again.

He sits on the bed and runs his fingers through my hair and says ruefully, "I'm sorry, baby, but I must go to work."

My heart sinks and I sigh. "I suppose I should too."

For a moment we let reality sink in, and I know this bubble has been burst and we need to drop back into life.

Flynn sighs. "I'll head back to Seattle with you and then I must leave for Canada."

"Why Canada?" I'm a little surprised at that and intrigued when he grins mysteriously. "To check in with my friends and report on a successful mission."

"What do you mean, mission?" I'm confused, and he shakes his head, his dark eyes flashing with excitement.

"I will tell you all about it but only when we have something to celebrate. All you need to know is that it concerns Winter and setting her free from that psychotic bastard she calls a husband."

For some reason I'm happy about that because even I could tell the poor girl was suffering. "Then make it soon, Flynn, because I have an idea her life depends on your success."

To my surprise, Flynn swoops down like a bird of prey and captures my lips in a deep kiss and God help me, I want him all over again. As he pulls back, he says fiercely, "I love you, Louisa Sullivan. Every day you astonish me by becoming even more amazing."

As he makes to stand, I pull him back and run my fingers over three rough scars that sit above his heart. I noticed them before and I'm curious about them and as I look up, his eyes gleam with something I can't put my finger on. "These claw marks were self-inflicted."

He sounds so casual, as if he's talking about a chest wax or something.

"Before we left college, Winter was taken and, for individual reasons, every one of us who lived with her was devastated. We made a pact to set her free and to earn membership into our select club, we used a claw shaped knife to pledge our allegiance with this scar, signifying where our hearts used to be. We had to park emotion aside, become callous and cruel and do what we must to set her free and change all our lives forever. This is what sent me to you, Louisa. This is what gave me my resolve to see this through and now I feel like a fraud because behind this scar is a beating heart full of love for you. Just imagining you in Winter's position makes my resolve even stronger to free her. So, Canada is a war briefing if you like. A mafia war where we regroup and plan our next step."

"Which is?" I am so in awe of this man, and he laughs softly. "I'm guessing it involves a trip to England for one of my friends. Let's hope he gets there before Massimo does."

* * *

A few hours later we touch down in Seattle. Then we take the short drive to my family home, and it's as if I've been away for months, not days. Vivian and my father greet us, and I can tell they are anxious about our meeting with my hated uncle.

I'm so happy for Flynn as Vivian pulls him close and warmly welcomes him home and as my father steps forward and hugs him tightly, the tears in my eyes are happy ones that everything worked out for him in the end.

As the night progresses, we tell them what happened, and it's so good knowing they accept us as a couple.

The funniest moment was when Sienna made an appearance and caught Flynn kissing me goodbye, and her shriek of disgust made me laugh out loud. I can still hear her saying, "That's gross. He's your fucking cousin, you maniac."

It was the sweetest moment to lift his hand and shake my head and say triumphantly, "No, he's not. He's my fiancé."

Her mouth dropped to the floor and for the first time in her life she was speechless and as Flynn left for Canada, I enjoyed every moment of telling her just how happy he makes me.

CHAPTER 38

WINTER

I have seen Massimo angry before, but nothing like this. We swept from the Capital Room like a cyclone, and I was fearful of what he would do next.

As I sit beside him in the black armor-plated car, he appears deep in thought, and I know better than to distract his attention from that. Hell, I try my best to keep his attention from me, but that's not always possible. If he's had a hard day, he likes to take it out on some poor unfortunate chained to the wall in one of his many dungeons. If they aren't available, it's my turn to step up and the more time that passes, the more I'm not sure I can cope with it.

As he silently fumes beside me, my thoughts return to Flynn, which is the last thing I want. I have trained my mind to shut them out. Pretend they don't exist, the men in my life who I would kill to protect. But it's becoming increasingly harder and seeing Flynn sitting opposite me with a woman who looked so much like my friend Emma, it catapulted me back to a happier time when the only thing I worried about was what would happen after graduation.

I stared down at my plate rather than catch his eye, but they burned into me the whole time. He sounded so self-assured and so together, which surprised me because out of everyone, Flynn found the madness hardest to deal with.

Just hearing his story broke my heart, and it was so painful not to react to that. Pretending to be concerned for Massimo is a tribute to my acting skills, which I credit to one person only. My son.

Everything I do is for him. My suffering is bearable because of him. I exist because of him, and I will not fail because of him.

The brief number of times I have been allowed to visit with him are the best memories of my life and I live for those moments.

One day I will set us both free, but I can't see how.

What terrifies me the most is that one day I will be seated at the same table in the Capital Room, or one very similar and Alessandro will be sitting across from me holding the hand of the woman he loves. It plays constantly on my mind that we will come across him and I hate that I hope he's alone. Just picturing him with someone else tears me apart, and when I look into Frankie's beautiful eyes, there is so much of Alessandro there.

Part of me hopes I never see him again and yet my heart tells me he is another reason for me to fight. He deserves to know he has a son. Meet him, love him, and protect him. If I can't be part of that, I will be happy for them. If I fail and my life is ended by the crazed madman beside me, all I hope is that Frankie is with Alessandro, who will love him as hard as I do. Don't ask me how I know that, I just do and as I caress the treasured memory of him deep in my heart for my pleasure only, I sense my resolve hardening. I can survive this hell on earth. There will be an opportune moment, as Baron told me, and I will kill Massimo Delauren and set us all free.

"You did well tonight, Winter."

I'm brought back to my reality as his hated voice cuts through the silence and I breathe a sigh of relief.

"Thank you, darling."

I project the emotionless voice he loves to hear, and he turns and grins in the dusky light of the car.

"Tonight, you may visit your son."

I'm sure my whole face lights up as I smile so hard, I think I will burst, and he laughs softly.

"Yes, you may sleepover in the nursery tonight because I have a long night ahead."

His features twist into a violent rage and he hisses, "It's time to show my best friend what happens when you betray me."

Normally I would pity the poor unfortunate soul in his sights, but for the first time since coming here, I wish I could be there. Just remembering what that man did to Flynn and his poor mother makes my blood boil like an erupting volcano and it must show in my eyes, because Massimo laughs with pleasure.

"My little wild cat. How I love to see the devil in your eyes, my dear. Perhaps I will let you observe your master at work. Maybe change my mind and cancel the sleepover."

He laughs even harder at my frantic expression and reaches over and grabs my face in his hands and squeezes it so hard it makes the tears spill from my eyes.

He leans forward and his foul breath sears my senses as he whispers, "But I need no distractions tonight. My perfect little doll will be a mom tonight and then tomorrow I am considering bleaching your hair."

He releases my face and shakes his head. "Now you have made me mark you, my darling."

He brushes against my soft skin, looking pained. "I will repair the damage with makeup before you can visit your son. You must be perfect at every hour of the day and night because you know what happens when any of my possessions are soiled?"

I shiver with fear because Massimo likes everything to be always perfect. If he senses a speck of dust in a room, it is completely renovated. If a crumb spills to his floor, he orders a new carpet or rug and I've known him to have the tiled floor pulled up and re-laid with new if anything splashes onto it.

Massimo is so afraid of imperfection it always surprises me how much he adores his hobby where he tortures, maims, and kills his victim in the cruelest of ways. Perhaps that's why he has the dungeons. He likes to enter them naked and there is a shower placed outside that he uses to wash their blood and internal organs from his body.

I imagine he would be a fantastic case study for any shrink, and I hope that one day he gets what he deserves.

We return home and head straight to my dressing room as we always do, and I am resigned to the routine by now.

I wait for instruction, and he says smoothly, "Remove your clothes and stand on the pedestal."

I have done this so many times it's no longer embarrassing and as he prowls around me staring at my naked body, I keep a blank expression on my face and act like the living doll he desires.

He makes me sit and brushes my hair one hundred times before applying moisturizer to my body and face. Then he slips a satin nightgown over my shoulders, followed by a matching robe. I step into satin pumps and as he takes my hand, he smiles happily. "Perfect. Just how I like it - for now, anyway."

I am always conscious I have a shelf life and sense that day approaching like the grim reaper sniffing out another damned soul.

As the door to Frankie's nursery closes behind our captor, I waste no time in rushing to his crib and staring hungrily into his angelic face. He is getting bigger every time I see him. As I watch him sleep peacefully, his long lashes brushing against his flawless skin, I physically ache to hold him. But he looks like an angel, and I would hate to disturb him and so am content with just inhaling the soft sweet smell of innocence in the middle of hell. Frankie is the lucky one. For now, anyway.

He has a full-time nurse and is cared for like a prince. No expense has been spared, and he has everything a baby could wish for except one thing. His parents. He exists in a gilded cage as yet another one of Massimo's playthings, and there is so much hatred burning deep inside me for the stolen minutes of watching him grow.

He stirs in his sleep and a small cry escapes his lips and as quick as a flash, I reach for him and hold him close against me, loving how sweet he smells.

As he snuggles into my chest and I hold his delicate head against me, I weep tears of love and frustration that all we are allowed are these stolen moments.

We retreat to the nursing chair and I hold him carefully in my arms, while singing him a soft lullaby to send him off to sleep. I have never felt such pure love for anything before and I will use that love to give me the strength to see this nightmare through to the bitter end.

CHAPTER 39

WINTER

Twelve hours of pure pleasure is over, and I was collected from the nursery and delivered to the dressing room by one of Massimo's guards. None of them can talk because he cut their tongues out years ago. They never even look at me. Just silently guide me to my cage, where I wait for the puppet master to pull my strings.

As always, I stand naked on the pedestal and sometimes stand here for hours. I'm never cold because Massimo keeps an even temperature in the room, but I know better than to move an inch because he watches from the cameras set up at every angle. I am his living doll to dress, play with and discard at will, and this is my shelf. He likes to dress me in the finest clothes, drip the finest jewels from my body and paint a masterpiece on my face. His comment about bleaching my hair raises my curiosity because he has always said how much he likes my hair to be as black as the night so he can see it shine.

The door opens, and he heads inside and my flesh crawls on my body as if it has a will of its own.

"Morning, my darling. I trust you got some sleep because today we are going out to play."

I say nothing and wait for the details and as he decides on what to dress me in, he tells me where we're heading.

"Iris Young was my nanny and like a second mother. It was her who raised me to be the strong man I am today."

He pulls a flowery sundress from the hanger and lifts a pair of white espadrilles from the shelf. Then he selects a white blazer before removing some white shades from the glass fronted drawer.

As he pulls out the most beautiful silk lingerie, I steel myself for his probing fingers to do their worst and as he runs those hands across my entire body, stroking, rubbing and kneading my flesh, I try to stand as still as a statue while he finishes the job.

"Yes, it's about time you met. She will be so happy to see I have a loving wife at last."

He fastens the bra around my back and drops a light kiss on the back of my neck and it takes all my concentration not to flinch under it. Despite the degrading way he treats me, it's never sexual. He isn't interested in me for that because he prefers young men. But hearing he has a daughter makes me wonder about his past and I am intrigued to learn more about the woman he obviously loved once upon a time.

I am soon ready, and he walks around me critically before snarling, "Iris has betrayed me. She tricked me and conspired with my best friend to keep something important from me. Today she has the opportunity to make up for that and so, Winter, my darling, I am bringing you along to watch what happens when my treasured possessions go against me."

He twists his mouth into a satanic grin and takes my hand.

"Shall we visit Mother, my darling? She will be ecstatic to meet you at last."

* * *

Cedar Heights is like a grand hotel and as we pass through the gates, I see a pleasant home set in parkland. It looks expensive, which doesn't surprise me because Massimo likes the best of everything.

We are met at the door as our cavalcade rolls to a stop and the woman standing there looks impressive in her navy-blue suit and crisp white shirt. Her hair has been pulled into a bun and she stands to attention with a huge smile on her face as Massimo helps me from the car.

"Mr. and Mrs. Delauren, welcome to Cedar…"

"Mrs. Travers, I have a serious complaint."

Massimo's word come out like rapid fire, and the blood drains from her face and her lip trembles. "I'm sorry sir, please tell me so I can put it right."

He snarls, "You allowed my mother visitors against my strict instructions."

"Visitors?" She looks confused.

"A few days ago, apparently."

He sweeps past her into the entrance hall, and she follows behind, saying in confusion, "I was away for one day. Perhaps they came then, and my manager forgot to mention it. We had to deal with a mild heart attack, and she may have forgotten about the visit in all the confusion. I'll enquire into it, and it won't happen again."

She is almost panting as she runs to keep up and he shouts so loudly it makes me jump. "NOT GOOD ENOUGH MRS TRAVERS!"

He turns on her shivering form and growls, "I pay you well to follow my rules, and this is your mistake. If anything has happened to my mother because of your negligence, I will make you pay. Do you understand?"

The madness in his eyes is scaring me and she is no different as she sobs, "Please sir, I didn't…"

"Leave us." Massimo nods to one of his guards who moves between them and as we continue on, she is guided in the opposite direction.

I walk quickly and silently beside him because when Massimo is in this mood, there is no point in trying to communicate with him. In fact, he may already have forgotten I'm here and as he heads for the unfortunate Iris Young, I am fearful for the frail lady who will be on the receiving end of his temper.

However, I'm shocked when he knocks gently on the door and enters the room, calling out softly, "Mama, I'm home."

A surprisingly firm voice says sharply, "Massimo, you're late."

He looks a little worried, which confuses me further, and as he stands before her meekly, he nods to me to follow.

Feeling like two naughty children before the principal, I stand with him as she peers at us from over her spectacles.

"Who is the girl?"

"My wife, mama."

"Your wife is dead."

Her harsh words cause him to flinch, and he says in a shaking voice, "My second wife, Winter."

Iris Young looks closer, and I see a stern woman with harsh angular features looking at me with derision.

"She's not good enough."

Massimo looks worried as she spits, "Nobody will ever be good enough for my son."

Now I'm even more confused because she was his nanny, not his mother, he already told me that, but they obviously act out a role they are happy with and I'm guessing she was more like a mother to him than his own, anyway.

She lifts a brush from the side and says sharply, "Kneel before me."

I am shocked when he meekly does what she says and as I

stand there awkwardly, she proceeds to brush his hair with a firm hand that looks quite painful.

"Tell me your news."

As she goes about her task, he says in a gentle voice, "I had dinner with a visitor of yours."

She hesitates before carrying on and says harshly, "I don't know what you are talking about. Make sense, Massimo, don't pretend."

I stare at him intently and see the malevolence creep into his eyes as he hisses, "Wesley Vasquez's son and my brother's daughter."

"Dimitri's daughter don't be ridiculous. Why would she come to see me? Stop telling lies, Massimo."

I jump when she cracks the brush hard against his head, causing it to lurch sideways and as he rights himself, the rage settles over him like a welcome friend, transforming him into the monster he is most of the time. As she raises her hand to carry on brushing, he grabs her wrist and turns, leaning forward so he is staring into her startled eyes.

"Are you lying to me, mama?"

For the first time, I see the genuine fear in her expression and her voice quivers as she says, "No."

The brush drops from her frail hand as his palm presses firmly against her mouth and her eyes water as he whispers in a voice dressed in darkness, "Now listen to me, you old hag. I have treated you like a loving son. Paid for you to live like a queen and been your only visitor for several years. There is nothing I wouldn't do for you and in return, I expected your loyalty."

I'm not sure if she can even breathe as her face turns red, and he snarls, "You betrayed me, mama. You lied to me, you took my daughter from me and put a cuckoo in the nest. You conspired with my best friend to lie to me, and I will never forgive you for that."

I'm not sure if she's still breathing and then he removes his hand, and she gasps for air.

Grabbing her head in both hands like he did to me, he snarls, "Where is my daughter?"

Iris's eyes are wide and frightened, and I pity her despite what she's done. I really hope she tells him what he needs but she looks defeated as she whispers, "I can't."

I have to admire her balls because Massimo is holding her life in his hands literally and yet if I were in her position, death would be a welcome compromise because it doesn't look as if she has that many years left, anyway.

"Why not?" Massimo's words are without emotion, despite the fact he is full of it right now and the tears leak from her eyes as she whispers, "I don't know."

"Try again." He tightens his grip, and she chokes. "All I remember is she went to England to a family I used to work for. Mr. and Mrs. Cruickshank."

"Now we're getting somewhere." Massimo sounds triumphant, and she says sadly, "They were killed in a car accident when she was one year old and the last I heard she was put up for adoption."

I am so fearful right now because Massimo has turned so red it looks as if his blood is about to boil over and he releases her and pushes her back in her seat. Then he paces across to the window, looking as if he's deep in thought.

For a moment I stare at Iris Young, and she returns it with a fearful one of her own and I'm guessing we are thinking the same thing right now. She is about to experience the extent of his anger, and there is absolutely nothing either of us can do about that.

The seconds tick by and then Massimo reaches into his pocket and pulls out a small metal box. I watch intently as he removes the lid and takes out a syringe, filling it with liquid from a phial nestling beside it.

I hitch my breath and stare at Iris with fear, but she merely looks resigned to whatever he has planned.

He moves back before her and drops to his knees and then a low wail shatters the silence. He sounds like a tortured animal hoping to be put out of its misery. Then he rests the syringe on the floor beside him before reaching for her and proceeds to hold her tenderly against his chest.

As my eyes rest on the loaded syringe, Baron's words come back to me when he told me to wait for the opportune moment.

This could be it.

As Massimo loses himself in the moment, I could step forward and plunge the syringe deep into his neck. I could save us all because I'm guessing there's nothing good about what's inside that phial.

A brief second is all I have and as my limbs respond so do his and he reaches out and wraps his fingers around my only chance before I can even move, and I watch with all the pain of a lost opportunity as he drives the needle deep into the back of her neck.

He openly weeps as she convulses in his arms and he whispers, "I'm sorry, mama. I love you, always remember that."

I'm shocked when he yells angrily, "Winter, sound the alarm! My mother is having a stroke."

Springing to the alarm pull by her side, I pull it hard and hope that help arrives soon, and they can do something to save her and as the footsteps pound toward the door, Massimo coolly pockets the evidence as he holds his former nanny in his arms, crying as he begs her to hold on. As the room fills and they put into practice a well-rehearsed drill, Massimo watches keenly the entire time, holding my hand.

We wait until the ambulance arrives and the medics check her over. As they hook her up to various lines and move her limp, frail body to the stretcher, one of them says kindly, "Are you her son?"

Massimo nods. "Will she be ok?"

"I'm not sure. It looks like a stroke. We'll know more when we get to the hospital. St Cedars, if you want to meet us there."

"Of course."

Massimo sounds every inch the concerned relative and as they whisk Iris Young away, we start walking slowly to the waiting car.

Once inside, Massimo leans back and says sadly, "Strokes are a terrible thing, Winter. The person could be locked inside their own body in a living hell. My poor mama, she will never be able to talk again. Never be able to spill my secrets and will be kept alive by tubes and drugs until I decide to pull the plug. Such a terrible end for a powerful woman, wouldn't you agree?"

The ice chills my heart with every word he speaks, because Massimo's revenge is a sadistic one.

As the car moves away, he sighs heavily. "Such a shame that I will be forced to re-home mama with us when this place shuts down when the murder investigations involving Mrs. Travers begin. Such a wicked woman dealing in death by being well paid to end her resident's suffering for money. What a tragedy, wouldn't you agree?"

I can only agree as we speed home, and all hope is left back at Cedar Heights. I am a fool if I think I can ever escape this despicable monster which is reinforced when he says brightly, "At least I will have my old friend Wesley to comfort me in my darkest hour. I'm afraid I have no further use of you for the time being, so you must return to the shelf. But stay strong, my dear, your day will come."

My shelf, as he calls it, is a white painted cage set in one of his dungeons where I live until he decides to play with me. I am not often locked in there, only when he has something that gives him way more pleasure to occupy his time, and I'm guessing the unfortunate victim this time is Wesley Vasquez. For once, I'm glad to be off the hook because even locked in a cage in a damp prison is better than the fate awaiting Wesley Vasquez.

EPILOGUE

CLUB MAFIA

*I*t's good to be back.

My private plane touches down on the small airfield close to the clubhouse, and I'm looking forward to catching up with my friends. When I travel here, I travel light and only four of my soldiers accompany me. Silvio has naturally stepped up as my consigliere and is much happier for it. Nobody admired or cared for my uncle, and it was an easy transition to shift allegiance to me. I am one of them, after all, and have lived a cruel life alongside them under his leadership. Not now though. Now I'm in charge and it's as fucking amazing as I always knew it was.

As I step into the waiting car to deliver us to the large fortress hiding in the wilderness, I lean back and close my eyes, loving that the madness has diminished in them. I can only give one person credit for that and thinking of Louisa safely at home in Seattle, heading back to work for her father, results in a peace I'm not accustomed to. It's good knowing she is waiting for me. That I am not on my own anymore. I have a family, a good family who love one another and surprisingly include me in that. My future wife is strong, sexy and powerful and so beautiful it strikes me awestruck every time I look at her.

Now I have a business, a mafia business, and it's up to me to make this life as safe as possible for all of us. So, here I am at Club Mafia, ready to touch base with my fellow dons and set in place the plan to guarantee our success.

The car stops short of the huge door that welcomes us inside and I sense the eyes of the guards watching from every lookout point. Angelo's men, who are loyal to him, guard him like the king he is and as the door opens, I see his consigliere Roberto watching us approach warily.

Silvio murmurs, "Hasn't he replaced that fucking dinosaur yet?"

I laugh softly. "He's an old woman but a loyal one. Angelo appreciates his experience and goes easy on him because apparently, he's clinging to life with his last finger."

"Aren't we all, sir?"

Silvio's dry retort makes me laugh and as I step up and nod coolly to Roberto, I prepare myself for a reunion of the most welcome kind.

My men drop back and retreat to their own lookout positions, like a well-oiled operation that seems so natural.

I follow Roberto to the great hall where Angelo will be waiting. That at least is guaranteed, and I wonder who has made it here before me.

Roberto opens the door and announces in a hard voice, "Don Vasquez, sir."

As I head inside the room, two men turn and clap slowly as I approach, and for some strange reason, it moves me a lot.

Stepping into their hugs, I am pleased to see Angelo and Malik are as emotional as I am and as we hug as a group, Malik whispers, "Good job, Flynn."

I nod because for some reason, I can't form words and Angelo slaps me on the back. "Two down, three to go."

We pull back and they regard me keenly as Angelo says with amusement, "I understand how you feel right now, Flynn, and it's a good one."

I nod. "The best."

"And your angel?"

Malik looks curious and then laughs as my eyes light up and I can't prevent the shit-eating grin from revealing my feelings regarding her. "Perfect in every way."

Angelo nods and grins broadly. "I also know how that feels. I'm happy for you, brother."

Malik groans. "Well, good for you, but some of us are still residing in hell and seeing the two of you wrapped in domestic bliss isn't making it any easier."

"Your time will come." Angelo reaches down to a table beside him and hands me a crystal tumbler of whiskey and they raise their own in a toast. "To Club Mafia and the next stage of our plan."

I glance around. "Where are the others?"

As if on cue, the door opens and Roberto shows in an enraged looking Beast and I share a guarded look with the others as he growls, "I need a drink."

Angelo lifts another glass of whiskey from the tray and hands it to him, which lasts all of a second before Alessandro sighs, "I needed that."

"What happened?" Malik's eyes narrow and Alessandro sighs heavily. "This shit is getting to me. The waiting is the hardest."

I glance at Angelo because the two of them share the pain because whereas Winter is Angelo's twin sister, for some reason during the short time they spent together, Alessandro fell deep and hard for the beautiful angel that is currently chained to Satan's side. As I peer closer, I see the pain has deepened in Alessandro's eyes and I'm worried for my friend.

Although he doesn't live with the madness of mafia the

same as the rest of us, he is still the heir apparent, and his grandfather has only allowed him to pursue his Hollywood dreams as a producer on the proviso he will succeed him as the head of the family when he dies.

Angelo says wearily, "Then you will be pleased to discover that phase three of our plan is already underway."

We all grin because this is big news and Angelo looks at Malik and says smoothly, "Maybe you should explain where Ivan is."

Our fifth member is missing, and it's not a surprise when Malik says with a great deal of amusement in his voice, "I finally got a location on Massimo's daughter. Her name is Charlotte Richmond, and she is currently locked away in her final year of finishing school deep in the English countryside."

"Good work." I'm impressed and Alessandro says urgently, "What's the plan?"

Malik exchanges a dark look with Angelo, and I recognize the evil gleam in his eye as he laughs softly. "We begin a race of the darkest kind. I'm guessing Massimo will find out the same information as I did, if he hasn't already and will be on his way to claim his lost daughter. It's just lucky that our Bratva friend was already in the country, and we have sent him to collect."

"Then what?" Alessandro is keen to act, and I feel so bad for him and yet relieved that he has yet to witness the suffering Winter is currently going through because I'm doubtful he would be able to hold back if they were in the same room together and our carefully laid plans would erupt in a bloodbath.

Malik says smoothly, "She is about to be kidnapped by a savage and we should spare a thought for the poor girl and the nightmare she is about to endure."

This makes us laugh because Ivan's nickname is well deserved. He is the only one of us who loves this life, revels in it and adores every sadistic moment of it. He loves to fight and the only man who can match him is our beast Alessandro and just thinking of the tattooed warrior heading Charlotte Richmond's way makes me expel a breath and say with meaning, "The poor woman. Born to a madman and about to be kidnapped by one. I'm sorry for her."

The others laugh and Angelo grins. "You would understand a lot about living with a madman. Tell us your story."

As I fill them in on what happened to get us to this point Malik whistles slowly. "Good work, Flynn, I'm happy for you."

I stare at him with interest. "How are things for you?"

The demons circle as Malik shrugs. "The same, but I will have my day. Have no fear of that."

Alessandro interrupts.

"So, the plan. Finish your story."

Malik nods. "Ivan removes Charlotte from life and keeps her hidden. We wait for Massimo to lose his shit when he can't find her and then go to him with a deal."

"We wait!" Alessandro's face is like thunder and Angelo says quickly, "We wait until the time is right. We have come so far, Alessandro. We are not about to go charging in and ruin everything. These things take time, and your involvement is needed to set Winter free more than anyone's."

"Then what are we waiting for?" Alessandro's eyes flash with malevolence, mixed with impatience and I almost pity him when Angelo says darkly, "We need your grandfather and his army for this to work."

As we all stare at Alessandro, the realization sinks in and I watch the defeat settle around him like an avenging angel claiming the soul who got away. He looks down and I wonder what's running through his mind right now and as he lifts his face and looks around the group, I see a gritty determination that wasn't there before.

"Consider it done."

There are no words to offer to make this moment any better for him because we all know what Angelo has just asked. Gone is Alessandro's freedom. His right to live a normal life. Now he must step up and return to his family. The most powerful Sicilian Mafia feared by every family in the world. Alessandro's grandfather is the head of that and if he is going to grant us any favors, he will only accept a very good reason for that, and Alessandro is going to have to offer him the gift he has been waiting for.

His soul.

* * *

Thank you for reading Club Mafia–The Angel
The next book in the series is
Club Mafia – The Savage

If you want to know what happened at Rockwell Academy read Club Mafia–The Contract.

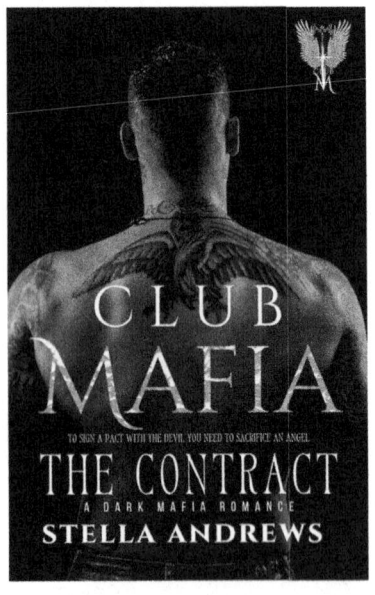

If you haven't read Angelo's story
Club Mafia–The Boss

Thank you for reading this story.
If you have enjoyed the fantasy world of this novel, please would you be so kind as to leave a review on Amazon?

Join my closed Facebook Group

Stella's Sexy Readers

Follow me on Instagram

Carry on reading for more Reaper Romances, Mafia Romance & more.
Remember to grab your free book by visiting stellaandrews.com.

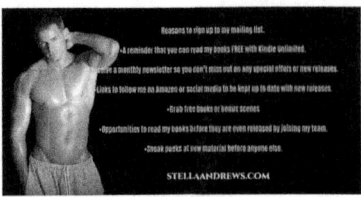

ALSO BY STELLA ANDREWS

Twisted Reapers

Sealed With a Broken Kiss
Dirty Hero (Snake & Bonnie)
Daddy's Girls (Ryder & Ashton)
Twisted (Sam & Kitty)
The Billion Dollar baby (Tyler & Sydney)
Bodyguard (Jet & Lucy)
Flash (Flash & Jennifer)
Country Girl (Tyson & Sunny)

The Romanos
The Throne of Pain (Lucian & Riley)
The Throne of Hate (Dante & Isabella)
The Throne of Fear (Romeo & Ivy)
Lorenzo's story is in Broken Beauty

Beauty Series
Breaking Beauty (Sebastian & Angel) *
Owning Beauty (Tobias & Anastasia)
Broken Beauty (Maverick & Sophia) *
Completing Beauty – The series

Five Kings
Catch a King (Sawyer & Millie) *
Slade

Steal a King

Break a King

Destroy a King

Marry a King

Baron

Club Mafia

Club Mafia – The Contract

Club Mafia – The Boss

Club Mafia – The Angel

Standalone

The Highest Bidder (Logan & Samantha)

Rocked (Jax & Emily)

Brutally British

Deck the Boss

Reasons to sign up to my mailing list.

- A reminder that you can read my books FREE with Kindle Unlimited.
- Receive a monthly newsletter so you don't miss out on any special offers or new releases.
- Links to follow me on Amazon or social media to be kept up to date with new releases.
- Free books and bonus content.
- Opportunities to read my books before they are even released by joining my team.
- Sneak peeks at new material before anyone else.

stellaandrews.com

Follow me on Amazon